I0674917

DRACULA SUCKS HOLLYWOOD DUDES

First Edition

Published by The Nazca Plains Corporation
Las Vegas, Nevada
2008

ISBN: 978-1-934625-66-8

Published by

The Nazca Plains Corporation ®
4640 Paradise Rd, Suite 141
Las Vegas NV 89109-8000

PUBLISHER'S NOTE
Dracula Sucks Hollywood Dudes is a work of fiction created wholly by *Tim Desmondes'* imagination. All characters are fictional and any resemblance to any persons living or deceased is purely by accident. No portion of this book reflects any real person or events.

Cover, David Farrugia
Art Director, Blake Stephens

DEDICATION

This book is dedicated to you much maligned but gentle class of vampires who live among us and serve us so unselfishly. I lift a cup of blood and salute you.

DRACULA SUCKS HOLLYWOOD DUDES

First Edition

Tim Desmondes

TABLE OF CONTENTS

INTRODUCTION

Immortality.

There are only two species who are immortal – who cannot die.

There are gods, of course. In any religion, the gods do not die. Or, if they do, they resurrect. And thus are immortal

And there are vampires. Many of them never die. There have been a few who were impaled through the heart, of course. And some of the more careless ones who got stranded in sunlight became defunct.

But prudent vampires never die. And are thus immortal.

There are many Romanian folktales that inform us about vampires. Some of those falsely paint them as evil. Bram Stoker, in his novel *Dracula* took that tack.

You will not find any evil vampires, though, in Hollywood. Trust me.

I'll tell you about the Hollywood vampires.

DRACULA SUCKS HOLLYWOOD DUDES

CHAPTER ONE

FANGS A LOT

THE VOICE OF TIMOTHY AXELROD

Maytime in Hollywood. Summer break in Palo Alto. Saint Judas Cyrianus Day at Mailamunte Castle.

Everything conspired to give me what promised to be the summer vacation of my life.

I was putting the finishing touches on the thesis I was writing for my master's degree at Stanford. I was up to my eyeballs in the research for that thesis: Transylvanian Myth and Folklore. One of my suitcases was stuffed to the brim with my typed notes and Xerox copies of pages from over forty documents. I now had three months of freedom from classes to pull the thesis together before my next term and a session with my departmental advisor.

I had always spent most of my vacations from Stanford at home. That is to say, when on break, I slept most nights in my bedroom at my parent's home on Padre Terrace in Hollywood.

Part of any break back to Hollywood always included a date or two with Carol Giurescu at the Eleutheria. Carol is his given name. His parents were Romanian immigrants who settled in Ohio. Carol is a perfectly good Romanian boy's name. It is probably not easy for boys with names like Carol, Leslie, or Jean to survive the taunts of the bullies in their early school years in an English speaking milieu. So Carol kept attempting to get people to call him Carl instead of Carol. But his actual name always seemed to emerge somehow. And when it did, he became an object of ridicule.

Carol came to Hollywood right out of high school, took acting classes, and very early on was signed up by Olympic Studios for character parts. Even though slight of build, he was very adept in tough guy parts. He had been the victim of bullies and could play a bully with a vengeance. Gangsters, bad cops, monsters, vampires, sleazes – he could play them all convincingly.

He took the screen name Karl Tepes. Karl was who he had wished to be as a kid. With a "C" or a "K." For Hollywood, "K" was a better choice for the parts he played. The "Tepes" last name was a nod to one of the nastiest characters in Romanian history, Vlad Tepes, a.k.a. Vlad the Impaler, and Count Dracula, among others.

Within the breast of this "tough guy" was the heart of a woman. Carol had always loved dressing in female clothes. In his younger years, his father found him in his sister's clothes three times. Carol was beaten severely for each of these transgressions. He had to be kept home with "stomach aches" after each beating until the welts disappeared.

Once away from home, and with a secure job in Hollywood, and with a large population of transvestites living in West Hollywood, Carol could indulge his feminine core while being seen on the screen as despicably male.

By coming to Hollywood, Carol/Karl had transported himself to Heaven.

He was my friend as Karl. And he was my lover as Carol.

From the time I was eighteen, I took pleasure in playing chess with Karl at times and with fucking Carol at others.

It was with Carol, at age eighteen, that I discovered that I love to swing both ways. I found plenty of lovers of both sexes when I went to Stanford. But, to date, Carol is the only actual transvestite I have fucked. And he always satisfies.

My sexual role is, and has always been male. I cornhole. I do not get cornholed. My cock gets sucked. I do not suck cock. Always the male role, because I am male to the core.

Carol had telephoned me before summer break to tell me that I should arrange my schedule at home during summer vacation around three dates. She had scheduled a room at the Eleutheria for May second. She said it could be just an evening romp or an over-nighter, depending on my schedule. In either case, it would be an evening of sexual fulfillment with a special fantasy theme.

For May third, she had arranged for me to meet a friend of hers who could furnish me with information that would enhance my thesis on Transylvanian myth and folklore. That interview was to be held at a bar in West Hollywood at seven in the evening.

The third date, May fourth, Saint Judas Cyrianus Day, she and I were invited to a grand party that, she said, would blow my mind.

Carol had whetted my curiosity, but would not reveal any details.

"You have to be here," she said. "One thing will lead to another. I guarantee you we will not only have a ball, but as a result of the experiences of these three days, you will have data for your masters thesis unavailable any other way."

I knew that Carol's parents were Romanian. Romanian had been her first language, since it was spoken exclusively at home when she was growing up as a "he." I guessed that she had some visiting Romanian lined up for me to interview, and even party with. Probably a Transylvanian. It promised to be fun and educational.

May Second, Eleutheria

I got home the end of April and spent time with my folks, my uncle and aunt, and with my old neighborhood buddies and girlfriends. My folks knew I had plans for the evenings of May second, third, and fourth. No problem.

I met Carol at the Eleutheria at eight in the evening on the second of May. The Eleutheria is a kind of exclusive hotel up in the Hollywood Hills for unconventional lovers.

When I entered the room Carol had reserved at the Eleutheria I burst out laughing. Carol was already there, as I knew she would be. But she was made up and dressed as Mihaila, Dracula's bride. Can you imagine walking into a room to be embraced by a stunning female Vampire? It started the evening on a fantastic fantasy note.

As Karl Tepes, the actor, Carol had played second and third banana in all four Dracula movies Otto Caruthers has made at Olympic Studios. As everyone knows, Lazslo Bocskay always played Count Vlad Dracula in those movies and Rozsa Katona played his voluptuous mistress, Mihaila.

Tilly Blaine, an old friend of my family, was the costumer for all the Dracula movies made at the studio. Karl had managed to borrow Rozsa's vampire dress from wardrobe with Tilly's help. Tilly knows all about Karl's transvestite side, Carol. No problem there. The wig and makeup were also right from the studio. Carol looked, to me, like a much more believable Countess Dracula than Rozsa ever did. But then, I'll admit to being prejudiced. I have never fucked Rozsa Katona.

There was my lover, Carol, in full vampire drag. The falsies beneath her bra were somewhat more voluptuous than Rozsa's natural cans. Her fangs perhaps dripped a bit more catsup. In short, she was more comic and yet more seductive than Rozsa.

I made her take out the fangs before we kissed. Her tongue ravaged the inside of my mouth while her left hand, with its three-inch claw-like nails roamed spider-like up and down the contours of my prick. She pulled away from our kiss, slipped her fangs back into her mouth, and, while continuing to fondle my rising dick with her left claw, nuzzled my neck with her fangs.

I thought it a neat beginning to the fantasy Carol had obviously given a great deal of thought to.

After the vampire embrace had run is course, Carol began to get me into character. Her makeup kit was on the table, so I knew I would get the vampiric white face with the black lipstick and black eye shadows. The formal nineteenth century formal attire, complete with cape, of course, was laid out on the bed.

Carol began to undress me, garb me in a vampire outfit, and apply my makeup. While she was doing so, I glanced around at the room setup.

The candelabra were the ones used on the set for Caruther's movies. Eerie with large dripping candles. The skulls that peered from every surface probably came from the studio prop department as well. A lidded coffin occupied a place of honor. I thought that was a rather nice touch at the time. The room was painted black. Madame Alexander, who runs the Eleutheria, can be relied on to re-do any room to fit the whims of her clientele. (For a price, of course.)

The furniture was all upholstered in black and the bed had black blankets but blood-red sheets and pillowcases.

My eyes took in the wetbar. I hoped Carol had not set up Bloody Marys for the occasion. We both enjoy Hollywood Tequila Sunrises as our *boisson d'amour.*

I was pleased. There were two bottles of El Tesoro Tequila Paradiso, one bottle of Guyot Crème de Cassis de Dijon, a gallon of orange juice, a bucket of crushed ice, and a cocktail shaker. Next to those there was a small mirror with a line of snow on it and a snorting straw. In addition there was a pot pipe with a dab of grass on it.

The cocaine was for Carol. I had tried that shit once. Never again. Carol digs it. Her business. The marijuana was for me. Two tokes max. Just enough to sharpen my sensations, not enough to overpower them. Party time.

Once I was made up and costumed I stepped to the full-length mirror, slipped on my fangs, and took in the sight. Honest to God, I did not recognize myself. I was ready to stay a vampire until the party was over.

While I admired myself in the mirror, Carol mixed the drinks.

(If you haven't been to Hollywood, here's the recipe for the Hollywood Tequila Sunrise. Place crushed ice into a cocktail shaker. Pour in two parts tequila and four parts orange juice. Shake but do not bruise. Strain into highball glasses. Slowly pour one part crème de cassis into each glass. As you drink, stir the drink from the bottom slightly at each sip , so the mixture varies with each swallow.)

We sat at the cocktail table. We had to take our fangs out to drink. That act made us laugh anew. I took a toke. She snorted. Time for the fantasy to begin.

I asked Carol whether we had names to match the characters we were portraying.

"Who would you like to be?" Carol asked.

I gave the matter grave consideration. A nobleman, certainly. A Transylvanian vampire nobleman. Not a count. The research I'd done for my thesis had assured me that Vlad Tepes Dracula was a Fifteenth Century Price of Wallachia and Transylvania. I certainly did not want to usurp his title. I knew Dracula could be quite unpleasant about such things. Perhaps I would be a marquis. I really didn't know what the Romanian equivalent would be for marquis. And, since this was all fantasy, marquis I would be.

"I am Marquis Timescu," I announced. "Are you my wife, my mistress, or just one of the girls?"

"That is yours to say, Marquis."

"Then I dub you 'Little Eva,' a newly fledged vampiress who must be taught and chastised by her master. What say you to that?"

"Yes, Master."

"Fetch me a bowl of blood, Wench," I ordered.

"By which Your Grace means a Tequila Sunrise?"

I slapped Little Eva. Not enough to hurt. Just enough to sting. Neither of us is much into pain.

"Of course, you stupid newbee. Go to the bar. Do not walk. Do not run. Fly!"

Little Eva fairly did fly over to the bar, mixed two perfect Sunrises, and brought them to me.

"Here, Master," she murmured. "Your blood cocktail."

"Why did you presume to bring two cocktails, you undead whore?"

Little Eva whimpered.

"I don't know, Marquis."

I took a mouthful of the cocktail and spit it into Little Eva's face.

"That's for you, Wench. The rest is for me."

Gee, this was a super fantasy. Carol liked a little humiliation. Not too much, of course. I knew that if I got too carried away, the fantasy would evaporate.

"You look distressed, Little Eva," I said, attempting to show disdain and compassion at the same time.

"I really would like a sip of blood, Master," she said.

"Come then. Kiss my cheeks and I may grant you a sip."

Little Eva gave me passionate, sucking and licking kisses all over my face.

"Slut!" I admonished. "Not *those* cheeks. Those other cheeks. Down there."

I stood up, dropped my trousers, and presented my ass to a somewhat surprised Little Eva.

She kissed not only my cheeks, but got her tongue into my butt-crack and even serviced my asshole.

When I had enough of that, I pulled my pants back on.

"That is a good vampire girl," I said. "Now you may have a drink of blood."

She reached for the cocktail glass she'd brought for herself. I slapped her hand away.

"No, you Fool Bloodsucker," I shouted. "You do not drink from the glass. You drink from my mouth."

I filled my mouth with Sunrise, pulled Little Eva's mouth to mine, and transferred half to her mouth while swallowing the other half myself.

In that fashion, we finished off both drinks.

"What now, Master?" she whined.

"You have had your fill of my blood," I announced. "If you are a true vampiress, you must now yearn for my essence."

"Oh, I do, I do!" Little Eva exclaimed.

"Then seek out the marquisial staff and fill yourself with the nectar of life eternal."

Grabbing the edge of my cape, I held it out to my sides like giant bat wings and strode majestically to the bed. I lay down with the cape still extended. It was the first time in my life I actually felt batlike.

Little Eva minced over to the bed and undid my fly. Right from the moment I took that first toke earlier in the evening, I had been sporting a real woodie. Little Eva had a touch of difficulty maneuvering that pulsating member out through the cockholes of my underwear and pants. But I didn't worry for a moment. Fantasy or not, I knew that inside Little Eva, Carol resided. And within Carol, Karl Tepes lived. And if any characters in Hollywood were skilled in getting a hard dick out of a pair of pants, that triumvirate of Eva-Carol-Karl was the ticket.

I did not care which of the three of them slipped a pair of moist lips over my expecting bulb. The expertise displayed was prodigious.

When I came, I ordered, "Drink down every drop, Slut. You know you love it.

I knew I was right.

We relaxed on the bed, drained and satisfied.

I'm not sure whether I dozed off or not. But I certainly was feeling satisfied with the world. After a while, I had kind of faded back into the scene and was aware that Little Eva was transforming herself back into Carol. She was sitting at the table in front of a mirror and was in the process of removing the vampire makeup.

"Who are you gonna be now?" I called out.

"Mihaila," was the one-word answer.

"Mihaila," I mused.

Mihaila, as mentioned before, was played by Rozsa Katona, Lazslo Bocskay's co-star in Caruthers' vampire comedy "Fangs A Lot." She's not much of an actress, but she can scream great, and she has hooters that look great in those black evening gowns she wears all the time in the movie.

The gown Carol had brought to the Eleutheria was high necked, unlike the ones in the movie. After all, those boobs in Carol's brassiere are falsies, so there's no way to give the effect of a convincing cleavage. That's simply a cross most transvestites have to bear. I'd been fondling Carol's falsies for years. No problem.

Now our fantasy was Marquis Timescu luring the virginal

Mihaila into not only a seduction scene but into one that transforms her into a vampire and ultimately, also, into Count Dracula's straight lover and also into Countess Dracula's lesbian lover. The movie is rated PG-13. No actual sex scenes. But the innuendo and double entendre of the script keep you laughing all the time. If you haven't seen it, get the CD. It's a scream.

So Carol and I were going to do a riff on "Fangs A Lot." I was gonna need another toke and another Sunrise to do justice to the romp.

Carol finished getting into the gown and into Mihaila's makeup and wig. She made up her face pale as death. She looked so luscious, and yes, even virginal, that I sprang a hardon just gazing at her.

She beckoned me over to the bar. I was, of course, still in my vampire attire and slunk across the room with that glide that Lazslo Bocskay patented.

Carol mixed and poured us our Sunrises. She took another snort. I inhaled a toke. And we were ready for our next fantasy.

My Uncle Mike, who's a set designer at Olympic, always takes me to the studio a few times when I'm back in Hollywood. So I was at Olympic when they were filming Fangs A Lot. Karl/Carol was already one of my lovers at the time, so I hung out around the set when several of the scenes were being shot. After the film's release, I took my dates to see the movie five different times. So I think I knew the lines nearly a well as Carol did.

In an adequate imitation of Rozsa's voice and Hungarian accent, Carol delivered Mihaila's lines.

"Oh, Your Grace," she pleaded. "Is it true that if I yield myself to you, my beauty shall never fade?"

"Your loveliness shall endure forever, My Dear," I replied, using Lazslo Bocskay's accent. Never mind that Dracula's family were all Romanian, not Hungarian. Ever since Bela Lugosi created the archetype of the silver screen count, Hungarian was the accent of choice for vampires.

"And, Count," she said.

"Marquis," I corrected.

"All right, damn it, then. Marquis. Is it also true that if I allow you and your wife to ravish me, I will live forever?"

"I must be honest with you, My Dear," I retorted. "You will not *live* forever. You will be Undead forever."

So far, we had followed the script fairly closely, with the substitution of Marquis Timescu for Count Vlad Dracula.

Mihaila now made what amounted to a costume change and what would have amounted to changing the plot from PG-13 to X-rated. She removed her evening gown, shoes, and hose, leaving her garbed only in panties and bra.

She threw herself onto the bed and panted.

"Then take me, Marquis Timescu," she pleaded. "Bite me, drain me, fill me with your essence of un-death."

You will recall, those were the very words moaned by Mihaila in the movie. At that point most of us in the audience always howled, and there were always a few who shouted, "Take her! Bite her! Drain her! Fill her with your essence."

I'll have to admit I was always one of those smartasses in the theater who chimed into that chorus.

Now, in that room at the Eleutheria that was decked out with skulls, a coffin, and a scantily clad transvestite writhing on the bed, it was up to me to improvise.

I had left my fangs on the dressing table. That would make the biting easier. I also left my shoes and socks behind. That left me in my formal garb, including the cape.

Now, where to begin the biting process? It seemed to me that the feet would be ideal as a starting point.

Karl/Carol/Mihaila is slight and delicate of build. She has legs that any genuine female would covet. Her feet and ankles are delectable. That was where to begin, for sure.

I began by biting her toes. Well, bite might not be quite the word. I gave each toe more than a nibble but less than a bite. A light enough clamp to leave an indentation on the skin. But not enough to pierce. Nothing that would need to be explained away the next day by Karl Tepes.

I made quite an antipasto of those toes. Emily's sighs and moans attested to the knowledge my bites were a propos.

Next I nibbled with the same light intensity up her calves and into that lovely morsel, the inside thighs. Here, I interspersed tongue and lip licks with the bites. I supplied enough saliva for both sighs to glisten with spit.

Emily kept her panties on, of course. The cache-snatch she wore under the panties kept Karl's peter disguised. I do not suck, lick, or touch male genitalia. I am not queer, you know.

With a deft shift above the bikini line, I renewed my biting-nibbling-licking-slobbering across and around Emily's intriguing abs. She sported a scrumptious six-pack for a chick. Hot damn! My boner was screaming for attention. I kept it in my pants but caressed it with my loving left hand.

Emily's bellybutton overflowed with the spit I administered to it.

With a quick snap, Emily's bra came off, and with it, of course, the falsies.

I'd faced this problem with my lover before. The chest with which I was now confronted was definitely not female. The pects were prominent. The owner of that chest obviously worked out at the gym and had developed those muscles well. But they were hard and muscular, not soft and voluptuous. But, what the Hell! A nipple is a nipple, isn't it? So I sucked, bit, and licked those suckers with tongue and lips. And I tweaked them with the fingers of the hand that was not entertaining my crotch.

As I approached her neck, Mihaila turned extended her neck and pleaded.

"Bite my neck and fill me, Marquis."

Mihaila had previously lubricated herself well with K-Y Jelly. Still wearing my cape, shirt, cravat and dinner jacket, I shed pants and shorts and took her and filled her with vampire essence while biting her on the neck.

In my passion, I could not hold back that bite as I had restrained it in my previous nibbles. I was aware that it was more of a true bite than a nibble. But not only did Mihaila not object, she pressed her neck into my teeth even as I clamped onto her jugular vein.

She was working her fingers under her panties and under the cache-snatch beneath them and arched in orgasm simultaneously with me.

Wrapped in each other's arms, we swooned on the red pillows in contentment.

We lay there in that embrace for quite a long time. She managed to slip the brassiere and falsies back on.

"Carry me to the coffin," she asked at length.

As I have mentioned, my lover, though strong, is not large. At Stanford, I had been on the racing crew three years and had done a bit of boxing at the gym. I work out and am strong and buff. So, carrying Mihaila from bed to coffin was not taxing to me in the least.

I encircled her body, carried it to the open coffin, laid it out gently, kissed her lips, and closed the lid. I noted there were holes on the sides of the box to let air in and out.

I sat on the bed and observed the closed coffin. Mihaila was now, according to the script, one of the Undead.

I was aware of a stickiness on my left hand.

I was about to wipe it off on the sheet when I observed the spot. It was red.

Red?! What the fuck!?

The red spot on my hand was not sweat or jism. There was no question what it was. Blood!!

I looked at myself in one of the full-length mirrors across the room. I saw a pants-less vampire. Unshod, bare legs, white shirt, cravat, dark circles around the eyes, black lips, and…red smears on the edge of the mouth. Red smears? Had Carol put those there when she made up my face? Or, was this still more blood?

I sat my bare butt on the bed and observed the coffin. There was not a sound from within. I told myself not to be silly. Fantasizing *Fangs A Lot* with my transvestite Transylvanian was playing tricks with my mind. Time to get a grip.

I listened for a rustle, a cough, or a deep breath. Deathly silence.

I opened the lid.

As I scrutinized more closely, I caught sight of her neck. There were two puncture marks with an ooze of blood on each one.

Was this testimony to my lover's adeptness with makeup? I looked more closely still. No. Those punctures were too realistic. They were right where I had bitten her.

I brought my hands to my mouth and checked my canine teeth. Had I bitten Emily that deeply? Had I grown fangs?

Emily did not move. Not a flicker. Not a twitch.

The goddam scene was over. Cut!

"Emily, arise!"

Nothing.

"Carol, get up and outta that coffin. God damn it!"

Nothing. Not a smile. Not a stir.

"Come on, Karl. That's enough!"

Karl Tepes' sepulchral voice ushered from within the coffin.

"Tim, My Boy. We have to talk!"

We did, indeed, have to talk.

"We have to get out of these costumes and take off our makeup." Karl said, even as he was sitting in front of a mirror and removing his Mihaila face.

I had to agree with him. If we were gong to discuss those puncture marks on his throat, I wanted us to be outside our fantasy world, with our feet planted firmly in reality.

I sat next to him and studiously restored my everyday face from the makeup.

When I saw the faces of Karl Tepes and Tim Axelrod staring back at us from the mirror, I was ready to remove all vestiges of vampire costumery. Off with the cape, dinner jacket, and cravat. Back on with Southern California casual.

When Karl had removed every bit of makeup, I scrutinized his bare neck. I was hoping the puncture marks would have disappeared under the vanishing crème.

Oh-oh! No way! He'd wiped away the blood oozes, but the puncture marks that appeared to have been made by fangs were still very much in evidence.

When we were both in clothes that would pass as normal on the streets of Hollywood and West Hollywood, we sat at the wet bar in the room. I certainly did not need more booze or pot. Karl eschewed tequila or a line. We sipped unadulterated orange juice.

"All right, Karl. About those wounds on your neck. Give!"

"You remember when I telephoned you while you were still in Palo Alto?" he asked. "I told you I had some surprises for you if you could get down here and make yourself available on May second, third, and fourth?"

"Do those marks on your throat have anything to do with the surprise?" I asked.

"You guessed it, Tim."

"Hit me first with the big picture, Karl," I urged. "We can get to the details later."

"Right," he agreed. "You know that thesis you're writing for your masters' degree?"

"Transylvanian Myth and Folklore," I stated.

"What are most of those myths and folk tales about?"

"You know as well as I do. The vampire myth."

"The big surprise, Tim, is this. Vampires are not myth. Vampires are real. As real as you are."

"You're shitting me," I answered.

But those fang marks on his throat made me wonder if my friend Karl, who I knew was of Romanian, even Transylvanian, descent, was not about to tell me that he was a vampire himself. Fantasy was one thing. But we had stepped out of fantasy into reality.

I hoped.

"I shit you not," he said, with his friendly smile that was not too unlike the leer he displayed in his vampire roles on screen.

"There are Undead dwelling in Hollywood," he declared.

I instinctively felt my neck to make sure I hadn't been fanged during our romp.

Karl laughed.

"Don't worry, Tim. I am not a vampire. And I did not bite you. And even if I had, and I repeat, I did not. But even if I had, it would not have turned you into one of them. That's not the way it works."

"Then what's with those puncture marks on your neck?"

Karl proceeded to tell me things my rational mind could hardly accept. If it weren't for the marks on his neck I would have scoffed. But I had to at least half-believe what he told me next.

He said that vampires had been living in Hollywood since the nineteen thirties.

"Vampires are no more evil than movie actors or college students," he claimed.

"Most vampires are quite nice people. They tend to be fun-loving, compassionate beings. They're not the kind of creatures portrayed in movies and novels. I really like them."

"Cut to the chase," I said. "What is *your* relationship to these 'good vampires'? What's with those goddam neck wounds?"

"I've met our local vampires," he admitted. "And I've exposed my jugular to a saucy hunk of a Nosferatu named Rock. Vampires classify humans into three groups: Mortals, Voevods, and Nosferati. You, Dear Boy, are a Mortal."

I felt my neck again. I looked at my reflection in a mirror.

Thank God, I was assured that I was, indeed, a mortal…still.

"Then, what are you?" I asked.

"I am a Voevod, at present," he answered.

"Meaning?"

"I let Rock sink his luscious teeth into my neck. That means that while I am mortal I can die even though I have received the Vampire Kiss. And if I should ever decide to become a Nosferatu, Undead, the path is now open to me."

Amazed? I was stunned. My friend and lover was sitting there drinking orange juice and informing me not only that vampires are real and living in Hollywood. He declared that he had been bitten by one, apparently voluntarily. And he had the bite marks to prove it. It appeared to me that he liked it.

"You say you *let* this vampire bite you. He didn't assault you and ravage your jugular?"

"Of course, Dear Boy. No one becomes a Voevod against his will. It simply doesn't work that way at all. The vampire myths were all written by superstitious mortals. You must ask, sometimes even beg, for the Vampire Kiss. And, if you should wish to become a Nosferatu, Undead, you need to convince a vampire of your sincerity."

I had been researching vampirism for over a year at Stanford. I had learned to read Romanian to get to secondary sources. I thought I was about as knowledgeable about the myths, folktales, ballads, and epics as anyone other than a few Ph.D.s What Karl was telling me did not fit in with the research available at Stanford's library and my explorations beyond academia.

"What in the world," I asked, "could have led you to let a vampire sink his fangs into your neck?"

"The sex, of course," he exclaimed. "The supreme sexual experience imaginable."

I had always felt there was a definite erotic undertone to all the vampire novels, plays, movies and many of the folktales. The very word "vamp" just oozes sex. Karl/Carol was, and is, a sexual connoisseur. What he was now telling me began to make some kind of cockamamie sense.

"Sex with a vampire, eh?" I said in as normal a voice as I could muster. "Tell me more."

"That is enough for now, Tim," he answered. "I promised you some surprises. What I've told you so far is enough for you to digest for the moment. My next surprise is for tomorrow night."

He paused to consider how I was dealing with his "surprises."

Apparently he thought I was emotionally prepared for his next bombshell. But, even so, he paused for me to tell him he could proceed.

I broke the silence.

"What do you have in store for me tomorrow?"

"A goldmine of information for a young man writing a thesis about vampires," he said.

"I believe your master's thesis is based entirely on what you academics call secondary sources."

"Right," I agreed. "Written documents about the subject."

"Are you up to dealing with a primary source?"

"Meaning a person who can give me direct, personal experience on the subject?"

"Exactly."

"Who would that be?"

"If you can deal with it, I know a one hundred percent, genuine Nosferatu who has agreed to meet you and be interviewed by you over cocktails tomorrow evening."

"Who?" I had to ask.

"Prince Radu Frumos Dracula."

The name Dracula threw me.

"Dracula?" I exclaimed.

"Not *that* Dracula," Karl laughed. "His brother."

"Dracula's brother?"

I was flabbergasted as well as intrigued. "Just how old is this vampire you say I can meet?"

"He was born in 1438," Karl said.

Karl did not appear to be joking. He was serious.

And I thought he must be nuts.

"So," he said. "Do you want to meet him or not?"

"I wouldn't miss it for the world," I enthused.

Nutty or not, I had to see what this was all about.

"Great," Karl said. "Tomorrow evening, at seven, meet me at the Transibar in West Hollywood. Prince Radu will be there."

He told me how to get to the bar. It is on Alta Loma Road. There is no sign on the building. There is only a gate with a dragon symbol on the door. I would have to find the dragon myself. The venue is only open to seekers.

I was excited and somewhat shaken. But I assured Karl I would find the bar and meet him and his friend who was over five hundred years old. I doubted that I would encounter anything that could be used in my thesis. I didn't want to get kicked out of college for academic heresy. Or because my lover was a loony.

But whether my lover was sane or deluded, I had to check this story out.

CHAPTER TWO

DRINKS AT THE TRANSIBAR

May third, Transibar

I arrived in West Hollywood about six-thirty in the evening. I gathered that finding the Transibar might be a bit of a challenge.

I wondered about the name of the saloon. Transibar. Located in West Hollywood, it certainly could refer to trans-gender. If Carol hung out there in drag, that derivation would certainly be appropriate.

On the other hand, the name could be a play on Tran-sylvania. If vampires, or Romanians, or clowns dressed up like vampires went there to get soused, the derivation would also work.

From the name, then, I didn't know what kind of people I would encounter. What I did not expect was a five hundred year old Transylvanian. Other than that, I was prepared for just about anything.

I drove the old Honda Civic up one side of Alta Loma Road and down the other. I was looking for some kind of dragon sign or symbol.

I couldn't spot a thing.

Finally, in desperation, I parked the Civic and got out to tramp up and down the street. I began to get exasperated. I came to the conclusion Karl was playing a big hoax on me. Who ever heard of a bar you couldn't find easily?

I continued my quest anyway. I walked up to every building, no matter how unlikely, to see if there was any kind of dragon displayed on it. It was approaching seven o'clock and I was getting pretty pissed at Karl. He was probably sitting down at the Abbey Coffee House on Robertson laughing his ass off at my wild goose chase. If I didn't find a Transibar soon I would go down to the coffeehouse, take Karl to a motel and fuck his ass off for this.

It was just a couple of minutes before seven when I hit paydirt. I cannot tell you anything about the building with the dragon sign. That is forbidden. Let me just say that the venue was unlikely. There was a small brass plate, not more than four inches high and three inches wide. Engraved on the plate in deep black was what I later learned was the dragon device of the Dracula clan.

I pushed open the door and stepped into what appeared to be an ordinary cocktail lounge. The décor was art deco. The dominant colors were black and gold. The people at the bar looked perfectly ordinary and were not dressed up like movie monsters.

There were both booths and tables in the room.

Karl was sitting in one of the booths with another person. He got up when he saw me enter. We walked towards each other and shook hands.

"Tim," he said with a welcoming smile. "I was sure you'd find the place. It is purposely difficult to figure out where this place is. The Undead are very insistent that no one approach them who is not sincere about seeking them out. Come. I'd like you to meet the prince."

He led me to the booth. The person sitting there arose, looked me in the eye, smiled a beautiful smile, and extended his hand.

"Your Highness," Karl said. "Allow me to introduce my friend Timothy Axelrod."

"Charmed," the prince said as he shook my hand.

"Me, too," I stammered.

I certainly was not prepared for Prince Radu Frumos Dracula. He was a stunningly handsome youth. That is, he appeared to be not much older than in his late teens. He was very pale, with longish blond hair, not quite shoulder-length. He was clean shaven. He was not dressed in evening attire and cape. Rather he wore a perfectly tailored Armani suit, tan colored with brownish stripes.

The guy was supposed to be a vampire who was more than five hundred years old? You've gotta be kidding.

We sat at the booth. The prince and Karl already had cocktails before them. A waitress, young, attractive, in cocktail dress, appeared immediately to take my order.

"The Cosmos here are prepared in classic Hollywood style," Karl said.

I could see that was what he was drinking, and ordered one myself.

My host certainly had features and bearing becoming an aristocrat. If he really was, or had been, a Romanian prince, I would test him just a bit. I leaned towards him and said, "Ma bucur sa va cunosc."

My knowledge of Romanian was a reading knowledge only. And at that time I still had to rely on a Romanian-English dictionary even at that. I knew the words for "Pleased to meet you," which I had just essayed. But I was far from sure about the pronunciation. As soon as I said it, I felt that I might have already made an ass of myself.

I glanced at Karl. He had spoken Romanian at home from the time he uttered his first spoken word. He didn't look particularly pained. He didn't show any reaction at all.

Prince Radu answered, "Multulmese foarte mult."

I was pleased that I understood that to mean "Thank you very much." And even more pleased that he answered as though I had spoken my line well.

I realize today, when I have a better mastery of the spoken language, that I had butchered the pronunciation very badly. But you would never have known it from the gracious way Radu responded.

I answered him, "Cu placere." *You're welcome.*

He'd passed the test. He apparently spoke Romanian. Now what?

"Would you mind if we spoke in English, Doctor Axelrod?" he said. "I need practice speaking your language."

Who was shitting whom? His English clearly was flawless. What he was doing was graciously letting me off the hook. It was clear to both of us that our conversation would be severely limited if it depended on my grasp of spoken Romanian.

"English would be fine, Your Highness," I said. "I do not yet have my doctorate, and 'Mister Axelrod' sounds stilted to me. Would you be comfortable just calling me Tim?"

"I would be delighted to call you Tim, Tim. And you must call me Radu. 'Your Highness' or even 'Prince Radu' feel *stilted* here in your informal Southern California. Wouldn't you agree?"

I agreed.

My drink arrived. It was a Cosmo, all right, the same color as Karl's. I glanced at Radu's drink. It was like the color of a Bloody Mary. Only deeper. Curious!

"Karl tells me you are a vampire. That is an astounding assertion," I said for starters.

"Our friend Karl is quite right. I am afraid we Nosferati have a very bad reputation. There are many false tales about my brother Vlad, spread by his enemies."

"Vlad being…?" I interrupted.

"The historical person who is called Dracula in folktale, novel, and cinema. Vlad is, of course, a Dracula. As am I. All descendents of my father, Dracul, bear the title and honorific of Dracula."

I knew enough Romanian to know that Dracul means dragon. It also happens to mean devil. And the descendents of a person called Dracul would be Dracula. I was kinda pleased with myself for figuring that out so quick.

"So your father, Dracul. When exactly did he live?"

"To begin with, my father's name was Vlad, like my brother. He was Vlad II, Prince of Wallachia. He received the Order of the Dragon from the Holy Roman Emperor Sigismund in 1431. That assured him the rule of the principalities of Wallachia and Transylvania. By virtue of that title, he became Vlad II, Dracul. And his progeny became Dracula. But, I am becoming too verbose. To answer your question about when my father lived, suffice it to say he was assassinated in 1447."

"I'm sorry," I said rather lamely. After all, the guy's dad died over five hundred years ago. Condolences hardly seemed in order.

"Karl tells me you are writing a masters' thesis about Transylvania," he said, changing the subject.

I was grateful that he didn't allow my dorkiness to hang out there over the table any longer.

"All I have are myths and legends about…"

I didn't quite know what word to use to finish the sentence comfortably.

"About us Nosferati, the Undead," he said helpfully.

"Well, yes," I acknowledged.

"To begin with, would it be helpful if I told you a bit of my own history?" he asked.

"I would be most interested," I said truthfully. "I really am quite curious."

"I haven't heard that much about your youth either, Radu," Karl said. "So I'd love to get educated right along with my academic friend."

"I would be most happy to oblige," he told us graciously.

He took a sip of his deep red cocktail. As he lifted his glass up to his mouth I tried to peer without staring to see if he had fangs. Damn! I couldn't tell. He appeared not to notice my rude scrutiny.

"My father, Vlad Dracul, had four sons. My father and his first son, Mircea, my older brother, were assassinated by henchmen of John Hunyadi, the so-called 'White Knight of Hungary.' My brother was fifteen years old when he was murdered.

"That left my father's other three sons, Vlad, me, and my younger brother, who took my oldest brother, Mircea's name, after the assassination. That younger brother later became a monk.

"So much for family history.

"The Turks were a threat, not only to our land, but to all of Christian Europe at the time. My father sought a truce with the Turkish sultan. As assurance that we Romanians would keep the truce, Sultan Murad demanded that my father send two of his sons to Turkey as hostages. Father complied and Vlad and I were sent to Asia Minor.

"That was in 1444. Vlad was thirteen and I was six. Vlad was very brave and protected me and comforted me on the trip to Turkey.

"Sultan Mohammed II, Murad's son, had not yet conquered Constantinople, so we bypassed that great city and were taken to Egrigoz in Asia Minor.

"Although Vlad and I were hostages, Egrigoz was hardly a prison. It was a palace at the foot of Mount Egrigoz (Egrigoz Dagi). There were about forty child hostages dwelling there, both girls and boys. I was the youngest when we arrived. The oldest was seventeen.

"We attended school within the palace five days a week. Classes were taught in Turkish, Arabic, and Greek. All of us learned to read, write, and speak in all three languages. Our education was worthy of royalty. Only the children of royalty were sent to the Turks as hostages.

"I liked the place a lot. The teachers were kind. There were lots of children to play with and there was lots of time given to us to play.

"Twice a week we spent the whole day without clothes. There was an upper gallery looking down on our quarters. The pashas, their wives, harem girls, male lovers, and harem boys gathered in the galleries on our naked days and sat up there watching us children romp around in the buff. Some of the older children engaged in sex games. The rest of us found that perfectly natural. When I was twelve, I enjoyed playing those games myself with the other more mature girls and boys.

"There were four hostage children who were with the rest of us only after sundown. They slept all day in a crypt. The rest of us were allowed to go down into the crypt if we wanted to. I went down a few times to see my friends. They slept in individual boxes from sunrise to sunset.

"We all knew they were called Vanijah. The word morphed into Vampire later in the West. The word Nosferatu had not yet been coined.

"The rest of us could volunteer to feed them when they arose from their boxes. The four would join us a little after sundown and feast on our blood. It was an experience I always liked. A kiss, usually on the neck, but sometimes on an arm or leg. The bite only hurt at first but then immediately it felt better than anything else in the world. Even better than rahat locum (rose flavored Turkish delight). I really liked to feed the Vanijah and early on thought I would like to be one of them myself.

"We all knew how to do that. You had to be at least seventeen years old. You had to convince one of them that you knew that you could only be out of your box at night, forever. You knew that your only nourishment would be human blood, forever. And that you would never age, but keep the way you looked then… forever!

"When you satisfied a Vanijah that you understood the consequences and still wanted to become Undead, one of them would release his retractable fangs, drink your blood until you had very little of it left, and then, through the fangs, release purakh into your veins to replace the blood. Then you were given your own box to sleep in during the day.

"The day I turned seventeen, I became Undead."

Radu paused and sipped his cocktail. He smiled at Karl and me. "That is a brief story of my youth. I hope I did not bore you."

"Not at all, Radu," I hastened to say. "Can you tell me about that fluid that converted you to a…vanijah?"

"Purakh," he informed me.

"That's the word," I agreed. "It's new to me."

"It is a Sanskrit word," he told us. "The earliest of our kind dwelt around Mohenjo-Daro, in the Indus Valley of what is now Pakistan. Archeologists find traces of them back to 3,000 B.C. But we know they existed there at least a thousand years before that. When the invaders from the Caucuses reached the Indus Valley, they imposed their language, Sanskrit, on the Vampiric culture. The Sanskrit word 'purakh,' meaning 'the bread of eternal life' was adopted to mean the substance we Nosferati can excrete through our fangs to grant the gift of eternal being."

Radu's explanation gave me glimpses into the ancient history of vampires going back into prehistoric times. Very interesting. But, at the moment I was really more interested in finding out more about his own history. Apparently Karl was, too.

Karl piped up, "Radu, I think we'd both be interested in knowing more about the life you and your brother lived after you'd been taken to Egrigoz."

"Life at Egrigoz was very sweet indeed," Radu smiled. "The strategy of the Turks was quite wise. As hostages, they held the princes and princesses of lands of potential enemies. They provided an environment for us which was designed to shape our minds favorably towards them, since we would be rulers in the countries we would return to. We were led to enjoy their sybaritic life style. I believe the term used today in your country is 'brain washing.' Well, I, for one, thoroughly enjoyed having my brain washed by the Turks. What was not to like? Sexually uninhibited playmates. The finest cuisine in the world, including sweetmeats that are, to this day, unrivaled anywhere. Music, games, sports. A very enlightened education incorporating the best of three cultures. The chance to play with vampires! Ah, you cannot imagine what pleasures lay there.

"I was enchanted by it all. I still am. But it was not so for my brother Vlad. By nature he is bellicose and rebellious. Quite the opposite of me. He was already a teenager when he was brought to Egrigoz. He was imbued with the concept that the Turks were our enemies. And he had been raised as a Christian.

"Vlad would not engage in sex games under the eyes of the sultan and the pashas. At night, when there were no spectators, he certainly had his way with the females. Most often he seduced them without resistance. Occasionally he forced them. Vlad had no interest in sex with boys. I always thought him weird in that respect.

"All the girls were taught the art of contraception before their flowering and thus were not inhibited by a fear of pregnancy. So Vlad enjoyed a sexual freedom while in captivity that would not have existed for him had he been a teenager back home in Wallachia and Transylvania.

"At age seventeen, in accordance with the terms of the rules followed by all civilized countries, Christian and Moslem, Vlad was free to return to our homeland. He returned most willingly. He had learned of the murder of our father and brother by the Hungarians. He had vowed to avenge those deaths. And, despite the education and attractive lifestyle he had been given by the Turks, he was very much the Son of the Dragon, a Dracula, whose destiny it was to be an enemy of Islam and protect the fatherland against any invasions of the Turks.

"When he left Egrigoz I was ten years old. Without big brother frowning on me, I could quite openly enjoy having the other boys and girls play with my penis. And I knew no better fun than playing with the sexual parts of the other girls and boys. It made no difference to me whether the sultan and his entourage were watching us from the balconies. I never tired of giving and receiving such attention to and from my playmates.

"Of course, when I reached puberty, I discovered brand new pleasures in sex. And when the Nosferati came out of the crypt to play with us after sundown, I could never get enough of the sexual pleasures that thrilled my entire being while getting my neck, arm, or leg fanged while engaging in sexual activity.

"My Undead playmates were frozen in seventeen year old bodies and sexual power forever. I envied that and knew that was the future I would want for myself when I attained that magical age.

"You may be wondering whether Vlad considered becoming Undead before his release from being held hostage. Not at all. He knew he could never attain his goal of revenge and military leadership if he could not operate during daylight. It was years later that he allowed the infusion of purakh into his veins. Perhaps more of that later, if you are interested. You asked to hear of my experiences, not Vlad's. So, to continue my story.

"In April of 1455 I was one month from my seventeenth birthday. All the hostages except some of the Nosferati left Egrigoz at seventeen. I would have liked to see Vlad again, of course. But Turkey really had become my home. I had been there since I was six years old, and neither my father nor my oldest brother were back in Wallachia any more.

"I remember distinctly that it was April 23 of that year that Ahmet, one of the chief eunuchs of the palace called me aside during a mid-morning rest period.

"'His Supreme Majesty, Sultan Mohammed, desires your presence at an audience in his chambers at five o'clock this afternoon.'

"Mohammed II had succeeded his father to the throne by then.

"What the sultan desired was what the sultan got. Mohammed II had conquered the great city of Constantinople two years before. He had re-named it Istanbul and was spending more of his time there than at Egrigoz. I had heard that he only came to Egrigoz as a refuge from the gigantic task of reconstructing the Graeco-Roman metropolis from a Christian capital to a Moslem one. I was astounded that he would want to take time from his relaxations at our palace to hold an audience with as unimportant a person as me.

"I naturally told Ahmet that I was most honored and would dress as appropriately as I could for the occasion.

"At four-thirty, Ahmet came to fetch me. I hoped I had made myself sufficiently presentable for the grand occasion.

"I was led upstairs into the adult quarters of the palace. And then up a further flight of stairs to the royal suites.

"Ahmet knocked three times on an ornate door. The door was flung open, and standing before me was an enormous eunuch in elaborate dress and turban with a drawn scimitar. He could have decapitated me in the blink of an eye. I very nearly lost control of two major sphincters.

"Ahmet told him I had been carefully searched, which seemed to satisfy the giant. I had occasion to be confronted by that enormous guard on future meetings, and even learned his name, Mustafa. But I was never comfortable in his presence. Nor was anyone other than the sultan intended to feel at ease when Mustafa was within view.

"Ahmet was left outside the door. Without a word, Mustafa led me to another door, this one more elaborately wrought than the previous one. He knocked twice. The great door flung open and a voice that carried great authority said, 'Listeye gir.'

"I had been taught the protocol from age six. I knew to drop prone on the floor and crawl face down on the carpet in a straight direction. I heard the door close behind me.

"The voice I knew to be that of Sultan Mohammed bade me arise. I sprang to my feet and stood tall and straight before the great man.

"The sultan was sitting on a golden throne. The throne was studded with precious stones and was bedecked with ostrich plumes that formed an enormous multi-colored fan behind him. He was dressed in a rich scarlet and black robe and wore an ornately decorated turban.

"To his right, seated on much less ornate thrones, were three of his wives. There was no mistaking their rank as wives. The costumes worn by rank in the Ottoman Court were well known to all of us who lived there.

"To his left, sitting on stools that were of gold, but un-embedded with precious stones, were three harem slavegirls. Again, their attire testified to their status.

"'You are Radu Frumos Dracula,' he said. It sounded more like an order than a statement.

"'I am, Your Supreme Majesty,' I answered in the bravest voice I could muster.

"'I have observed you from the balcony for a number of years. You are a most comely youth.'

"'I am honored to have you say so, Majesty.'

"'I have chosen you to perform a service for me,' he said. 'You are aware that no order of mine may be disobeyed.'

"'Of course, Your Majesty.'

"'Which is why I am not ordering you to perform this service. If you choose not to do so, I will not think any less of you and you may return to your quarters bearing the gift of the sapphire I hold in my left hand. If you choose to perform the service, you shall return with the diamond I hold in this box in my right. What I am telling you is that I am dealing with you as a free agent. You will be rewarded whichever choice you make.'

"'I am gratified by your kindness and consideration, Majesty.'

"'To my right, Radu Dracula, are three of my loveliest wives. All three, at present, are in their most fertile period. Do you understand what I mean by that?'

"'I have been graciously educated by the Ottoman Empire, Your Majesty. I understand well what is meant by periods of female fertility.'

"'It is my desire to have a prince of the Empire who is, in appearance, European. You see my three queens are fair of skin.'

"It was quite clear that these three queens were Arabian in

race, not Turkish. They were several shades lighter than the haremgirls sitting to the sultan's left. Those three were lovely indeed, but decidedly Turkish.

"'You are not only comely, Young Man, but exceedingly blond. I would be pleased if you would take each of my three wives to bed on three different nights. With three different women, one is likely to bear a son. When that son comes of age, he will be able to serve me as an ambassador to the West. He will be an Ottoman prince with a European appearance. I would like you to father that prince. You are, yourself, a Wallachian prince. As stud, if I may use a coarse term, to the queen, the result should be splendid.'

"'So tell me, Young Prince Radu. Will you choose the gift of the sapphire or of the diamond?'

"'Your Majesty is too kind and generous. And I would be honored to receive a diamond from your royal hand.'

"And with those words, I had three nights of royal coitus.

"Sultan Mohammed clapped his hands once. Mustafa the eunuch appeared at his side immediately, scimitar in business readiness. I must admit, his sudden appearance gave me quite a start. I had not been aware he was even in the room.

"The sultan ordered him to conduct me to a royal boudoir.

"Mustafa led me through a labyrinth of rooms to a suite that contained a throne similar to the one I had seen Mohammed sitting in before. In addition to the throne, there was a small round table with a drinking glass on it filled with a pale liquid. But the dominant feature of the room was the bed.

"It was built low to the floor and was enormous. The room itself was hardly small. And the bed occupied most of the room.

"'Undress,' the eunuch ordered.

"I complied.

"A Blackamoor slavegirl appeared from a side door.

"As I removed my garb, she silently received each piece of clothing.

"When I was quite naked, she minced out of the room with my clothes.

"I looked around and somehow Mustafa had also disappeared.

"I stood alone and naked in that room wondering what would happen next.

"The main door flew open and the sultan marched in accompanied by one of his wives and one of the haremgirls. He was still wearing his royal robes and his elaborate turban. The wife and the haremgirl were as naked as I was. I didn't see the giant eunuch anywhere around but I knew he was present somewhere in the room.

"Mohammed sat on the throne and the haremgirl kneeled on the carpeted floor facing him. The wife, whom I recognized from my previous audience with His Majesty, approached me.

"The sultan directed his attention to me.

"'Drink the kenevir sarap that has been prepared for you and that you will find on yonder table,' he invited.

"Actually it was closer to an order than an invitation.

"I had heard of kenevir sarap, but had never seen the drink before. It is an aphrodisiac wine that was available in Asia Minor during the entire existence of the Ottoman Empire. It has not been available anywhere in the world since 1923.

"During my years in Turkey, I seldom imbibed kenevir sarap. I perform expertly without it. Its effect is to prolong potency well beyond what is normal for a male, allowing orgasms with ejaculation for many hours. A vampiric kiss has a similar effect on mortals. And, of course, there is no need for aphrodisiacs for us Nosferati. Virility is one of the effects of the purakh that courses through the veins of male vampires.

"Fatima, for such was the queen's name, was absolutely beautiful. She was an Arabian with those Semitic eyes that are so very sensual. Her breasts were full and inviting with rosy protruding nipples that fairly demanded to be suckled. Her midriff gave proof that she had practiced belly dancing, for it had softly rippling muscles that promised voluptuous pelvic action during intercourse.

"Her mound and pubis were enticing and all but caused me to fall on my knees to nuzzle the delights they promised.

"In all, I could hardly wait to perform the duty that would earn me the diamond.

"Fatima extended the glass of kenevir sarap to me and, as

ordered or invited, I drained the glass. I felt an immediate surge of passion bursting in my midriff. The sight of her nakedness had already provoked my erection. The effect of the aphrodisiac was to cause my organ to pulsate and my testicles to tingle.

"I could not resist looking over towards the throne. Sultan Mohammed was still fully garbed in turban and robes. The bottom of his robe was now raised above his lap and the haremgirl was fondling the ruler's fully aroused member.

"I know you twenty-first century Americans cannot quite picture the supreme ruler of the grandest empire on earth sitting on a throne and being serviced in that way in full sight of a seventeen year old boy. It is probably impossible for anyone who did not dwell among the Ottomans to understand their absolute lack of modesty when it came to sexual pleasure. For that matter, all forms of pleasure were always paramount. I really miss the mores of that empire. Gone! Disappeared forever! I fear that Puritanism prevails around the globe in these times.

"Fatima guided me to the bed. She laid me down on it and ran the rounded orbs of her breasts on my body from chest to crotch. Her hardened nipples caused goosebumps wherever they grazed my skin.

"I was fully aware that I was being watched while I was engaged in this pleasurable pursuit. For years, I had been watched from balconies as I pleasured and was pleasured by my fellow hostages. That my audience was the supreme ruler of the greatest empire on earth did not faze me. It was not only my youth that served me. I had never really known any other morality than that practiced by the Turks.

"Fatima slithered up my body, her hands tracing gossamer trails up and down my genital areas. Her lips met mine and her tongue slipped into my mouth. My excitement was such that I had fear of loosing my seed into the open air. That would not do.

"I disengaged from the kiss to whisper in her ear.

"'If you wish my essence in your womb, we must engage very soon.'

"She responded by sitting upright, a knee on each side of my hips. Her sex was drenched with her natural aromatic effluvia. She settled her fragrant vagina over the knob of my penis and began a descent until I was completely swallowed within her waiting love channel. My seed flowed voluminously into her womb and a shudder of satisfaction convulsed both of us.

"Young friend," Radu smiled, looking first at Karl and then at me. "I don't believe anyone will fault me for what proved to be an ejaculation that was, if not premature, quite early in the engagement."

Neither Karl nor I was able to respond to that statement. After all. What could we say? "Sorry?" I don't think so. "That's all right?" Rather condescending to a being older than us by about half a millennium.

So we both just smiled back, hoping he would continue his history without responses from us mortals.

His story so far had given me a boner that required some adjusting since it was partly restrained by my jockey shorts. As nonchalantly as I could, I reached down into my pants and adjusted my equipment. It was, perhaps, a bit gauche. But the resulting comfort was worth it.

Radu apparently wasn't really expecting any comments from us. He sipped his drink (was it human blood? I wondered) and proceeded with his tale.

He addressed me.

"It has not been that long since you were seventeen, Friend Tim. So you can recall the short recovery time at that age from ejaculation to ejaculation. With fifteen to twenty minutes I would have been in priapic condition to sow more of my seed into Fatima's womb.

"However, I was given a somewhat longer respite for a nourishment break.

"The little Blackamoor came shuffling back into the room, this time bearing a silver tray loaded with oysters on the half shell. The point was for me to fill Queen Fatima's womb full to overflowing with my seed. It was believed at the time, the more seed in that receptacle, the more likely the conception. And the more likely the conception, the greater chance of the queen bearing a fair-skinned son.

"Oysters, fish roe, and peacock eggs were purported to replenish seminal fluid. I have discovered that there are even people living in your country at this time who hold similar quaint beliefs."

(I didn't want to reveal my own quaintness. But I believed in oysters and eggs myself at the time. I certainly did not intend to confess that to Prince Radu.)

His tale continued.

"A very sweet, very hot tea was in a pot on the tray. The Blackamoor placed the tray on the small table, poured the tea into a demitasse, and bowed to the sultan and to the queen. The curious maid then nodded to me and swept out of the room.

"I offered the refreshments to Queen Fatima. She declined.

"I observed His Majesty. He was contentedly being fellated by his haremgirl and was not paying any particular attention to me and the queen.

"I downed every oyster on the tray. There were about fifteen or twenty. I did not count. The tea was refreshing and may or may not have had aphrodisiacal powers. If it was a love potion, I did not need it. I was ready to release more of my seed into the royal womb.

"Fatima expressed concern that some of my seed that had erupted into her womb had spilled out of her vagina. We decided that on our next encounter I should be on top, her on the bottom, at the moment of climax. There might be less spillage that way.

"My phallus was beginning to burgeon again. She laid me back down on the bed and massaged my testicles with a balm she had at hand. She told me the massage would encourage the oysters to enter my jewel box and stimulate the growth of more seed. The balm emitted a most pleasant warmth to my scrotum and thence through my entire genital region.

"She then applied the balm to my phallus, which had bloomed into eager readiness.

"I requested Fatima to lie down beside me. I desired to play the traditional male role to the hilt. In our previous coitus, she had actually made love to me. This time I chose to make love to her.

"We heard a noise from the direction of the throne. It is hard to miss the sound of a man in the throes of a massive orgasm. The Grand Sultan of the Ottoman Empire was clearly expelling his royal seed into the oral cavity of his highly skilled slave.

"I smiled at Fatima. She smiled back. I encircled her smile with my own lips. My kiss was slow and languorous. This time, there was no danger of me wasting my seed in the air. I had ejaculated on the previous encounter and would thus be in much greater control of my orgasms for the rest of the evening.

"As our tongues played in-and-out games, I fondled her breasts with one hand and traced the gentlest of caresses up and down her exterior labia. The moistness I encountered down below was a mixture of my own residue and her own luxurious effluvia.

"I broke loose from the kiss and lowered my lips to her perky nipples. I brought my moistened hand from her crotch to her lips.

"She sucked the nectars from my fingers. I reached back to her crotch, scooped up more nectar, rubbed it on her nipples and sucked the flavored breasts with elation.

"Of all the flavors on this earth, none intoxicates me more than female love-juice and male semen. Not even blood which, as you must be aware, is my sustenance."

(I was almost sure of it then. The prince was drinking human blood from that cocktail glass even as he was spinning this incredible tale of his experiences back in 1455. I was not positive whether I was awake or involved in a bizarre dream.)

Radu continued.

"I was in full control. The queen's erotic excitement was quite evident. I had a hunger to lick my tongue around that lovely female jewel that lies behind the hood. I believe you Americans call it the 'boy in the boat'"

Karl and I nodded in agreement at the term and I may have even emitted a slight giggle.

Our host continued.

"My tongue played love games with her turgid love button. She squirmed, she sighed, she wiggled, she arched.

"The moment approaching climax had arrived. I mounted her, pumped, and pumped, and pumped a bit more as I tweaked her breasts. And, we orgasmed simultaneously. I felt sure that if I had not impregnated her previously that I had achieved that result as we spasmed together."

Radu paused and smiled as he recalled that blissful moment in his life that had allegedly occurred over five centuries previously. He took a sip of his cocktail and turned his smile on us. Karl and I smiled back.

"You must excuse me," Radu said. "I have rambled on about a rather personal experience, and have found myself entrapped in a sweet reminiscence. I will not tax your patience further with descriptions of the passionate exchanges that occurred between me and the three queens. There was sport aplenty as I fulfilled my duties as a stud for the Ottoman Empire.

"I was never informed whether Queen Fatima, Yasmin, or Karina bore the son the sultan craved. If not, it was not from any lack of enthusiasm on my part.

"The day after I had serviced Karina, the third of the queens, I was summoned to an audience with Mohammed II. This time the setting was not in the throne room but in the informal venue of one of his private bedrooms.

"I was conducted there by Ahmet and received by Mustafa.

"I dropped to the floor as before and began to crawl towards the sultan when he broke out in laughter.

"'For the sake of Allah,' he roared. 'This is a private meeting between the two of us, not a formal audience. Stand up, Radu. Walk over here and have a seat beside me.'

"I stood up, and looked Mohammed in the eye. He was smiling at me in a friendly way. I knew Mustafa must have been somewhere in attendance, but I could detect no sign of him.

"What I was aware of was that there was a new relationship between the sultan and me. He had watched me in carnal engagement with three of his queens, on three different occasions. I had observed him watching me in that endeavor while he was being openly fellated.

"The sultan and I had established some kind of new status. I wondered, though, just what that might be.

"He was seated on an elaborately wrought chair that though elegant was less than a throne. An identical looking chair was placed beside it. He invited me to sit there.

"'First, to take care of business,' my sultan began. 'May I complement you on a job well done over the past three evenings?'

"'It was a pleasure, Majesty,' I responded.

"We both laughed heartily as though we were equals.

"'I enjoyed your performance, myself,' he quipped. 'I love to watch sexual engagements. Particularly when I am being simultaneously engaged myself.'

"'My awareness of the pleasure Your Majesty was feeling added to my own pleasure. And hopefully enhanced my reserve of seed for the royal wombs.'

"My compliment was a success. The sultan actually clamped a hand on my shoulder as he gave way to a series of guffaws.

"'I promised you a reward,' he went on. 'In this rosewood box you will find my payment for your services.'

"He handed me a beautifully carved box.

"'Open it,' he urged.

"I opened the box and gasped. I had never seen such an object before in my life. I could tell it was a diamond. But I thought it must have been bewitched. It emitted multi-colored rays that, taken together, were a blaze of glory.

"Mohammed laughed that deep chuckle of his again.

"'It is, Young Radu, a jewel of great price. I believe it befits the services you have rendered to our domain. It is a diamond, but one subjected to a newly discovered art. The diamond, as you undoubtedly have been taught, is the hardest substance Allah has placed on our earth. It has been a treasured jewel for over fifteen hundred years. And, until now, it has defied faceting. But, recently, in a province called 'the low lands' at the western edge of Europe, artisans have learned to cut those facets you see, causing the diamond to catch a thousand rainbows within.'

"So, for my three nights of joyful coitus, I was rewarded with one of the first cut diamonds ever produced. To this day, it is my prize possession."

(I enjoyed Radu's story. But "one of the first cut diamonds ever"? Fucking the Ottoman queens? Born in 1438? I was beginning to smell bullshit. I suspected my friend Karl was part of a giant hoax being played on me. Then I looked at Radu's cocktail. The dude really *did* appear to be drinking blood. Or was he? How could I really tell what blood would actually look like in a cocktail glass? Well, whatever was going on, hoax or not, I found it entertaining and was willing to go with the flow.)

Radu continued with his tale.

"I was overwhelmed with gratitude and insisted that His Majesty was far too kind and generous. I asked him how I could possibly show my thanks.

"'Kiss me on the mouth as you kissed my queens,' he responded.

"I was taken totally by surprise. But if that was how he wanted me to show my gratitude, I was not at all averse. I got up from my chair.

"The sultan held his face up to mine and we exchanged kisses as passionate as those I had traded with his wives.

"When we had a fill of each other's lips and tongues, I resumed my seat. We stared into each other's face. I was fully aroused and I could discern that he was as well.

"Mohammed was not what you would call a handsome man. I know he was not as tall as I was. He was of swarthy complexion with a face covered by a beautifully trimmed black beard. So, although not a man anyone would call beautiful, he was the most imposing human being I have ever known. He exuded power, virility, and refinement. I had kissed and been kissed by the most powerful man in the world. And, I was in love. For the first and last time in my life, I had actually fallen in love.

"'You have found favor in my eyes,' Mohammed said. 'Within weeks, you will be seventeen years old and free to return to Wallachia and Transylvania. Or, of course, you can choose to remain in our empire. I invite you to remain with us if you like and become one of my companions.'

"I knew what he meant by 'companion.' For his sexual delectation he had three harems and one or two uzunsachs. There was the Royal Harem, which included his wives and official titled concubines. In addition there was his Slave Seraglio, with women collected for him from all over the Islamic world and beyond. There was his Juvenile Paizorium inhabited by pretty boy slaves imported from as far away as China and India.

The royal harem traveled with him from Egrigoz to Istanbul as he made his peregrinations from one palace to the other. He maintained separate seraglios and paizoria at each palace. His uzunsachs, or long-haired boys, were nearly always in his entourage. Unlike the slaveboys in the paizoria, uzunsachs were freeborn males.

"To be one of the young male lovers of the man I had fallen in love with seemed the finest fate that could befall me. I knew the sultan discarded his uzunsachs after a year or so and took on new ones. Fair enough. For as long as he would have me, I would be happy to be one of his lovers. I answered him not with a word, but with a passionate kiss.

"'Had you ever considered becoming a vampire?' he asked.

"He used the word 'vampyr' which had morphed from its Sanskrit origin 'vanijah' in much of the Islamic world.

"I admitted that I had desired that state, but would be willing to forego the metamorphosis for the present if that was his preference.

"He told me that he had observed me in evening romps with the vampires from the crypt. He suspected that I might be inclined to accept the status of the Undead.

"He said, 'I have had sexual congress with such creatures and have found it always to be excruciatingly pleasant. I would be delighted to have an uzunsach who could provide me with such delights.'

"It was at that moment that I agreed that I would become one of the Undead before my seventeenth birthday, and my entry into my new position as a 'long-haired boy.'

"In the early evenings, when the kids from the Crypt came out to play, I had formed a very close personal relationship with one of the most attractive vampires I have ever known. Sajillah was a hostage from the Mogul Kingdom of the India subcontinent. The Moguls were allies of the Ottomans, but each side, Ottoman and Mogul, distrusted the other. They exchanged hostages to ensure stability in their relationship. Each side sent two male and two female hostages to live in the other's domain for four years. The Mogul Rajah of Punjab sent his Undead daughter Sajillah to the Ottoman court three years previous. In the Islamic world at the time there was no fatwa against sending vampires as hostages.

"I had known Sajillah since her arrival in Egrigoz three years before. She and I had been playmates in every sense of the word. Before I had even had my audiences with Sultan Mohammed, I had convinced her that I wanted her to give me the gift of immortality before my seventeenth birthday.

"On May first, 1455, I spent the entire night in Sajillah's embrace. In the course of nearly eight hours of lovemaking, she sucked my blood from my body in small doses, inserting purakh from her own reserves into my awaiting arteries. I had experienced exquisite lovemaking previous to that night. And since then I have enjoyed pansexual pleasures beyond those known to any mortal. But the evening of my transfiguration remains the supreme experience of my being.

"Unlike most of my erotic experiences, that night did not include a variety of activities. There was no fellatio, no cunnilingus, no sodomy, and no masturbation. With Sajillah's fangs constantly embedded in my jugular, my lingam was firmly ensconced in her yoni. (The words lingam and yoni are taken from the form of Sanskrit Sajillah spoke.)

"Both she and I were in a state of orgasm from sunset to an hour before sunrise. An hour before the sun rose, the other vanijahs carried my newly transformed body down into the Crypt and placed it in an elaborate coffin the sultan had provided for my daytime repose.

"The next evening, May second, was my birthday of becoming Undead.

"I awoke that next evening aware that I had been moved from the Crypt. And I was fully aware of what I now was. The lid of my casket would open with a gentle push. But I wanted to remain in the dark for a while. I had become a creature of the dark. I wanted to revel in it.

"At length, I pressed upward on the lid and beheld the ceiling of the room I had been brought to. It had an elaborately decorated ceiling in tones of reds, blacks, and golds. There were no graphic representations of people or things. There *were* elaborate patterns of geometric figures with verses from an eleventh century Persian poet named Omar Khayyam written across the patterns. His quatrains had long ago been translated into Turkish and I had memorized many of them as part of my schooling. The beauty of the designs and the poetry filled me with an ecstasy I had never felt as a mortal.

"I now wanted to get out of my casket and discover whether the rest of the room would be as excitingly beautiful.

"My casket had been placed on the floor, so it was quite easy to extricate myself. As my feet met the carpeted floor I saw that the entire room was as gorgeous as the ceiling. But I ceased observing the room when I realized that I was not alone. There were two other people in the room, each enveloped in an aura. I blinked my eyes, and the auras disappeared, revealing that Mohammed II was seated on an elaborate chair smiling a radiant smile on me. Standing next to him, straight and respectful, was a handsome golden-haired youth.

"I blinked again to observe the auras. The sultan's aura's predominate color was violet. I instinctively knew this indicated a genuine caring for what he was observing. The violet was bordered by pink. This showed me he was joyful at that moment.

"The youth's aura was a bright red. He was clearly aroused sexually by what he was observing. The red was bordered by orange, the color of joy and warmth. He wanted to be friend and lover of the person he was observing.

"Sajillah had told me that I would be able to read auras when I became Undead. It was a further gift of the purakh. And an ability that enriches my life.

"I bowed to His Majesty, who held out his arms for me to come to him. He stood to embrace me.

"After a warm kiss on the mouth, he introduced me to the golden youth.

"'Radu, I want you to meet, know, and love Konstantinos. He is my daytime uzunsach. You are my long-haired boy from sundown to dawn. You two will share this suite.'

"It was a case of love at first sight. Not the kind of love I felt for the sultan. That was very deep, very emotional, and eternal This love for the youth was temporal, and based on sexual attraction alone. I had read his aura and knew that my love was reciprocated. We approached each other and kissed in greeting. Sultan Mohammed was pleased.

"'Konstantinos will be not only your partner in pleasing me and pleasing each other. He will be the source of your sustenance. He will eat and drink from the bounty of our court. You will feed on his blood. I have willed it, and it shall be so.'

I observed Konstantinos as this was said and could see that he had been blood-sucked before. And that he enjoyed it as much as I had when I was a mortal.

"In my newly acquired state, all my senses seemed to be heightened. I did not yet know whether the sense of physical pain would also be enhanced. I later discovered that we Undead do not suffer physical pain, but that emotional pain is still very much a part of our being.

"Mohammed stated that it would give him pleasure to watch Konstantinos and me make love with each other. Knowing the sultan's proclivities, I was not surprised. Voyeurism was a key element in his libidinous life.

"Konstantinos and I stood facing each other. In practically mirror image we began to disrobe. As I removed my tunic he copied my move. We tossed our tunics to the side, mine to the right, he to his left. I shot my shoe to my right, he to his left. Next came our undershirts. Bare-chested, we appraised each other. I very much liked what I saw.

"The Turks had not destroyed the statues left behind by the Greeks when Anatolia was conquered. Konstantinos, by name and appearance, was clearly Greek. He could have been a model for Praxiteles' statues of the gods. He was gorgeous. I blinked to observe his aura as he eyed me. The red of his aura glowed so bright it was nearly an assault on my senses. A lovely assault.

"Next came our trousers. His legs had the beauty of an athlete. His arousal beneath his underpants was as evident as I knew mine to be.

"Our final discard was our underpants. We stood in rapt attention to the allure of each other's penis. As a Greek, he was born a Christian, as was I. That meant that unlike the Moslems, we were both uncircumcised.

"Rather than shaking hands, we approached each other and took the other's turgid phallus by the hand for a greeting that amounted to a fondle.

"I thirsted for his blood as I had never before thirsted in my existence. He threw back his head to expose his neck to me. As I bent my mouth to that enticing vein I longed for, I experienced for the first time the automatic extension of my canine teeth. The sensation was as stimulating as the sprouting of a penile erection.

So this was how fangs emerge.

"I sucked his delicious blood up through my fangs as he pressed his flesh into my sexually stimulated fangs. He shuddered with erotic delight.

"His blood flowed through my fangs directly into my own veins. I knew, for the first time, that I would be able to discharge my purakh into his bloodstream as a kind of orgasm. I also knew that to do so without the consent of a lover would be an abomination.

"Konstantinos indicated through a movement of his body that he wished to turn away from me. I disengaged my fangs so he could do that. He turned about, and I re-sought his vein anew, with unerring success.

"As I continued to satisfy my blood-lust, my phallus entered his rectum. And in this position, we made love. I sodomized him while reaching around and simultaneously masturbating him.

We reached simultaneous orgasm.

"And that, my friends, was my first sexual experience as an Undead individual."

Karl and I looked at each other and exchanged smiles. Radu's story, if true, explained elements of vampirism that my researches had left me wondering about. But I doubted that I would be able to include any part of it in my master's thesis.

My lover and I sat there in a kind of stunned silence as we considered the tale we had just heard.

All three of us finished our drinks. The waitress returned to our booth with a tray of new drinks. I don't know about the others, but I sure did need another drink after having heard Radu's tale of his first experience of sex as a vampire.

When we had all three settled into our newly arrived cocktails Radu told us a bit more about his experiences.

He and Konstantinos accompanied Mohammed II on his continuous travels throughout his extensive empire. Istanbul, Izmir, the Mediterranean islands, inland to Ankara and beyond. New marvels greeted the uzunsachs as they visited most of the wonders of the world that had once been Greek, Roman, or Egyptian, but were now Ottoman.

As uzunsachs, Radu and Konstantinos had free access to the seraglios of sex slavegirls and paizoria of sex slaveboys. The royal harem was off limits, of course. That was the sultan's private domain.

When Mohammed did not desire his ministrations, Konstantinos amused himself by day in the seraglio and paizorium and Radu was an habitué at night.

During the hour or so after sunset when the two uzunsachs were up and about together, Radu fed on Konstantinos, always while taking pleasure in his body. The two were wont to go take in the delights of the seraglio or paizorium together, occasionally setting up the kind of orgies that had reigned in Constantinople when it was still a Christian city.

On occasion the sultan enjoyed a threesome with his uzumsachs. He was fascinated with his Christian uncircumcised boys. All his Moslem boys had been circumcised in accordance with Islamic law. To fondle the foreskins of Christians was a passion of his. A special delight for the sultan was to play with Konstantinos' prepuce while watching Radu masturbate by manipulation of his foreskin over his glans.

The romp always concluded with Radu sodomizing Mohammed while Mohammed sodomized Konstantinos who masturbated during the operation.

Radu told Karl and me all this in a very matter-of-fact way. Although Hollywood, in some ways, is the New Istanbul in sexual mores, we still consider the things Radu told us about to be somehow promiscuous. And promiscuity is considered nasty still. The court of Mohammed II would not have found a word in Turkish for "promiscuity." Sexual pleasures were simply a part of life, like food, drink, and recreation.

In somewhat less than a year, the sultan decided to replace Konstantinos with a young, handsome Turk named Recep. Konstantinos was given a villa in Izmir, the city that had been called Smyrna under Greek rule. Radu had occasion to visit his companion there later.

Radu had a somewhat longer tenure as the sultan's long-haired boy. His playmate and new lover Recep taught him a few new tricks that were practiced by the Turkish Janissaries. These all involved animals. Radu enjoyed the novelty, but gave up those practices when he left the sultan's sexual service.

In 1457, the sultan was ready to replace Radu. Mohammed dispatched him to the island of Samos, just off the Turkish coast. Radu was made governor of the island and inherited the governor's palace and his seraglio and paizorium.

Radu did not elaborate about his stay in Samos, which lasted until 1462.

In 1462, his brother Vlad was imprisoned by the Hungarians. Mohammed II needed Wallachia and Transylvania to be ruled by a puppet loyal to him. Radu was sent from Samos to Wallachia and ruled as prince there in his brother's absence.

Radu told us much more about himself and Vlad. None of the information went into the thesis I was writing. For those readers with a historical bent, I have summarized some of the history Radu related to us in Appendix I on page 121.

I was interested in learning about the superstitions that are held about vampires. I asked Radu about that.

"In stories and movies about vampires, there's always mention of garlic, mirrors, crucifixes…that sort of thing. Is any of it true?"

Radu laughed heartily.

"Many of those beliefs persist to this day among some of the peasants in my country," he replied. "Particularly within the minority Saxon community that resides there.

"The truth is that we *do* have a certain aversion to garlic. It is actually an allergic reaction. The purakh that flows through our veins and arteries is sensitive to garlic odor. Some mortals are allergic to strawberries, or ragweed, or other substances or pheromones. We Nosferati tend to be allergic to garlic. We avoid it when we can.

"It is also true that we are not fond of mirrors or other reflecting surfaces. The superstition is that we do not reflect in mirrors. That is quite untrue. We *do* reflect, and we cast shadows, just as you mortals do. But mirror reflections tend to give us headaches, so we avoid them when we can.

"There is also that ridiculous belief that crucifixes repel us. Totally unfounded, of course. Many Nosferati are Christian and venerate crucifixes. The idea that crucifixes are anathema to us originated with the Saxon minority in Romania. The Saxons are Roman Catholics. The Romanian Christians are Eastern Orthodox. The Orthodox shun the Roman version of the crucifix. All this religious bickering has spilled over into Saxon superstition. Religious bigotry fuels ignorant superstition quite readily.

"There is the false belief that we have superhuman strength. Not so, except in perhaps one regard. Male Nosferati can achieve multiple orgasms. Most mortal men cannot. If one considers repeated orgasm to be somehow superhuman, so be it.

"There is also a belief that we can read minds. I am happy to say that we cannot. However, we *can* see auras, and thus know the emotional state of mortals and Voevods. We also have heightened senses and see beauty in the world where mortals cannot. From the mortal point of view, I suppose that seems superhuman.

"Finally, there are those silliest of all beliefs. In novels and movies there are depictions of us turning ourselves into bats or wolves.

Sometimes we're even shown turning into mist or floating particles.

"Rubbish, of course. We are absolutely corporeal. Who in his right mind would want to turn into a bat? Disgusting."

When Radu paused and looked at us, I had the uncomfortable feeling he was reading our auras. Could he interpret when I believed him and when I had my doubts? Did my aura turn violently red when he frankly discussed his sexual relationships? Was he seeing more of me than I wanted to reveal?

I thought he could see my discomfort as I pondered these matters.

He attempted to set me at ease by introducing the subject of my thesis.

"Tim," he said. "This thesis you are writing for your university. Do you need any information about the historical origin of my kind?"

I told him I had never seen any reference material about that.

Radu gave me a short history of the spread of vampirism from its earliest days. The reader with an interest in history will find a précis of the information in II on page 125. The general reader is unlikely to care much about the subject.

The waitress returned with a new round of drinks. My interest in what Radu was drinking must have shone bright and clear. I could tell that the prince was studying the emanations that I now knew surrounded my body.

"My friend," he addressed me. "I fear that I do not have a great deal more time to chat with you. I have a few business matters to attend to while it is still night. But I perceive that you have had a question on your mind all evening. Something you hesitate to inquire about. I beg you not to shrink back in your quest for knowledge about my kind."

He had me dead to rights there. The question had nagged since the first round of drinks was served. What the Hell was the vampire drinking? I hoped I was blood. And I hoped it wasn't blood. If it was blood, I hoped it wasn't human. And I also hoped it *was* human.

And if it was human, where did it come from? Did he suck it out of his victims and then store it in jelly jars? Or what?

I knew it was no use lying to him. Vampire or not, he had convinced me that he could read my aura. So I might as well risk the truth.

"You know what my question is, Your Highness."

"Radu," he corrected.

"Radu."

"As you have perceived, I have no hesitation in answering any of your questions. But you must ask if you want to know. As a scholar you know the methodologies of research. If you want answers, you must pose questions. Is that not so?"

It was exactly what my advisor up at Stanford would have said. If I wanted to know what vampires, or people who claimed to be vampires, drink at cocktail lounges, I would have to pose a question or a premise.

I led into my question.

"Karl and I have been enjoying drinking excellently prepared Cosmopolitans this evening. My compliments to the bartender."

"I will inform him of your critique, Tim. He will undoubtedly be delighted."

I thought I detected more than a touch of irony in his tone. I had managed to avoid stating my question and deserved an ironic or even a sarcastic answer.

I tried again.

"Here is a premise I would like to test, Radu."

"Aha!" he replied. "The scholarly approach. I appreciate that. State the premise and we will explore it."

"The premise, which I draw solely from Romanian folklore and myth, is that vampires are sustained by the ingestion of human blood."

"I can tell you, as an authority on the subject, that in this case, folklore and myth have it right," he said. "Might I ask, however, that we substitute the word 'Nosferati' for 'Vampires'? It is currently the more politically correct term among our kind."

"Thank you for your answer and for the help on acceptable terminology," I said. "Accepting the premise to be true, might one postulate that Nosferati do not drink alcohol?"

"That would be too rash a postulation," he answered. "At this moment, do you believe there is alcohol in your own bloodstream?"

From the state I was in, I knew alcohol was not only in my bloodstream but was coursing through my brain as well. I got Radu's point.

"I understand that if a Nosferatu were to feed on me at this moment, he would imbibe alcohol along with my blood," I said.

I could not suppress a shudder as I talked about the possibility of fangs entering my neck. If Radu didn't see the shudder, he certainly read the color that must have emerged in my aura.

Karl giggled. The bastard knew damn well what was going through my mind.

I blurted out the question I had.

"All right, Radu. Let me be blunt in my question. While Karl and I have ben drinking with you, what was in your cocktail glass?"

"Blood," he answered sanguinely.

"Human blood?" I asked.

"Yes, human blood, of course."

"Unmixed?" I asked.

"Straight," he replied. "No vermouth or ginger ale mixed in it at all."

Radu smiled. Karl laughed. At some level, I was horrified and knew I showed it.

Still, I remained a stolid researcher. I pursued my questioning about the source of that blood. What blood types, if any, were most desirable?

His answers, while of importance to me, are unlikely to be of interest to the general reader. The reader who is of a scientific bent will find a synopsis of Radu's answers to these questions in on page 127.

Radu had given me more information about the Undead than I could have imagined even existed.

"You must excuse me, Gentlemen," he said in his courtly manner. "As I told you, I must go attend to business. Young friend Tim, Karl received an invitation to the Saint Judas Cyriacus Ball we will be hosting tomorrow evening at Mailamunte Castle. He asked at that time if you, his good friend, could join us as well. Karl is so dear to us that we agreed, even though we did not know you. Be assured that now that we are acquainted, you're doubly welcome."

I've already told you that Karl had asked me to keep May fourth open. The chance to attend a party with vampires, or people who thought or pretended to be vampires, was both forbidding and impelling. In the blink of an eye I responded.

"Thank you for the invitation, Radu. I would love to attend. What is the occasion again?"

"I leave Karl to answer your questions. You must excuse me. I mustn't be late for an important meeting with some of my associates."

"It has been such a pleasure to meet you," I expressed. "You have been most generous with your time and with the information you have imparted."

"You are quite welcome," he responded. "I look forward to seeing you tomorrow evening at the castle."

With that we all stood. And damned if he didn't have a cape draped over his chair. A cape with an Armani suit? Who was putting whom on?

But when he fastened the cape about his neck, the fucking thing matched. He looked great in it. A dude who looked like he was a teenager in suit and cape appeared perfectly natural to me.

I wondered if the Cosmos I had been drinking over the past several hours had anything to do with it? Or, perhaps I had fallen under a vampire's spell. A very good-looking hunk of a vampire at that.

Radu fairly swept out of that bar. Karl and I looked at each other and laughed. Why did we laugh? I didn't know then and I do not know now.

Karl and I sat down at the booth after Radu left. The waitress came over and asked if we would like anything more.

As I looked her over, I noticed for the first time that she had very pale skin. *You don't suppose?* Could *she* be a vampire? In the world Radu had described, might cocktail waitresses be vampires? He claimed to be a businessman and a prince. He had told me he owned the cocktail lounge and a couple of mortuaries. And apparently he had other business interests as well. Why couldn't other people who worked exclusively at night be Undead? Hollywood was full of night people, late night broadcasters, trashmen, policemen, whores…

Perhaps I had just never noticed that after sundown the real world I inhabited was swarming with vampires. I was tempted to ask the waitress if she was a Nosferata.

But instead, I only asked her for the bill.

"The bill has been taken care of," she said with a lovely smile.

I tried to get a good look inside her mouth. Did she have fangs? I couldn't tell. But then, I had learned that Nosferatu fangs are retractable, so I probably wouldn't have seen overly long and sharp canines even if she had them.

"I guess Radu took care of the tab," Karl said.

The pretty waitress cleared away the glasses from the booth and left Karl and me to talk.

"Tell me about this bash we're going to tomorrow," I said to my friend.

"May fourth is a big day for the Nosferati," he told me. "It is Saint Judas Cyriacus Day on the church calendar. You know how the Irish celebrate Saint Patrick's Day on March seventeenth? For the Nosferati, Saint Judas Cyriacus Day is kinda like that."

"Who the fuck was Saint Judas Whatsisface?" I asked.

"He's the patron saint of the Nosferati, of course. He was a very devout, saintly Frenchman back in the eighth or ninth century. He set out on a pilgrimage to the Holy Land. When he was passing through Transylvania…"

"Wait there!" I interrupted. "Don't tell me. When he got to Transylvania he was bitten by Dracula and became a vampire. Patron saint of the goddam Vampires! It *that* what you're gonna tell me?"

Karl laughed.

"He wouldn't have been bitten by Dracula, if it's Vlad Tepes you're talking about. Wrong century. But, yes. Judas Cyriacus met the Nosferati in Transylvania. He ministered to them, willingly became transformed into one, did good works, worked miracles, and later was martyred and canonized as a saint."

"How the Hell can you martyr a vampire saint?" I asked.

"The Saxon minority that lived in Transylvania at the time were still pagan. And…"

"I get it," I said. "The old wooden stake up through the asshole, right?"

"You got it, Pal," Karl said.

"I sure as shit hope not," I rejoined. "Remember, Karl. I'm not the one who takes it in the ass. You are."

We were drunk enough to think that was hilarious.

"What's gonna happen at the party?" I asked. "I'm not gonna get the old bite on the neck, am I? I don't think I'm up to a neck-job."

"There'll be three classes of people at the party," Karl answered. "There will be other mortals like you who have never had the Nosferatu Kiss."

"The neck-job," I quipped.

"Yeah," Karl answered. "Although the bite isn't always on the neck. It can be on the arm, or thigh, or just about anywhere blood can be drawn.

"There'll be Voevods like me at the party. We've had the experience of being fanged while we were being fucked."

"And the other group present at the shebang will be real vampires," I hazarded.

"At the party you might try referring to them as Nosferati," Karl corrected.

"Right!"

"All three groups will intermingle until midnight," Karl continued. "For the mortals and the Voevods, there's champagne and canapés. The champagne is always vintage La Grade Dame from Veuve Clicquot in France. Unlimited open bar, but champagne only. The Nosferati are very fond of La Grande Dame in the veins of their lovers when they suck."

I'd had champagne a few times at New Year's parties. It was all cheap bubbly made here in California. I didn't particularly dig it. I hoped the vintage crap from France would be better. But, what the Hell! If that's what they would be serving, that's what I would be drinking.

"I don't suppose the Vam…Nosferati drink the champagne the

way we mortals do," I guessed.

"Were you listening to Radu at all?" Karl asked.

I got the point.

"Up until midnight," he continued, "it's a regular ball. There'll be music, dancing, smoozing…"

"If it's a Hollywood crowd," I interrupted, "there'll be gossiping for sure."

"Of course," Karl continued. "Then, about eleven-thirty, chimes will ring. Those chimes will be telling the mortals present that they are advised to leave within a half-hour or so. Because, starting at midnight…"

"The sucking begins," I interjected. I couldn't help myself.

"Exactly. When you're at the party after midnight, it means you expect to get sucked."

"In the neck," I put in.

"Or elsewhere," my pal said.

We both thought that was funny as Hell, too, and laughed our asses off.

"So," Karl said when we had caught our breath. "We had better go to the party in our separate cars. I'll be staying on. You probably'll want to leave before…"

When he hesitated I blurted out, "Before the sucking and fucking begins."

That one knocked us both out. We thought it was so goddam hilarious.

It was agreed that we would meet at the gateway to Mailamunte Castle at eight the next evening.

(For those interested you will find information about Mailamunte Castle in Appendix IV, page 129.)

Karl asked me if I would like to come to his place for the rest of the evening.

To tell the truth, I really did not feel like fucking Carol that evening. I didn't allow myself to dwell on what my plans were for later. But they did not include making love to Carol's ass.

I begged off with some lame excuse about my parents expecting me back at their place to watch TV with them. It was a crock and Karl knew it. But he let it go. I suspect that his invitation was as half-hearted as my refusal. No big deal.

We staggered outta the joint and headed for our individual cars.

Neither of us should really have been driving. But I got to my folks' place in one piece and managed to get to the bathroom without stumbling. And from there I managed my way to the bedroom that had been mine from infancy.

From the bathroom I'd grabbed a couple of Kleenex to take with me to my bedside stand. I knew I would be needing them.

I looked at my old bed. I was flooded with nostalgic thoughts. When I was thirteen years old, I'd had my first wet dream in that bed. I'd been dreaming about Elsbeth Ziegenfus, a sixteen-year-old babe who lived two doors down. She'd grown a pair of knockers that absolutely fascinated me. I never let her know she turned me on, of course. The age difference at that time in our lives was a chasm.

The jism residue in my pajama pants from that wet dream was an embarrassment the next morning. I tried to rinse it out so my mom wouldn't know I'd had the experience. That was a major plight of puberty.

About six months later, in that very bed, I couldn't get to sleep. All I could think of was Elsbeth and her tits. I pictured her floating naked over my bed with her gorgeous boobs hanging down over my face. My hand went to her cunt. Her hand was on my cock.

But, whoa! That wasn't her hand. It was mine. And it was doing a job on me that I couldn't resist.

Not into my pajama bottoms again! No! Where was my pocket handkerchief?

I managed to get to my hankie and came into it. *There* was a memory for me. The very first time I jacked off. But hardly the last. I will never forget it.

Here it was ten years later. I was in the same bed, this time drunk as a skunk. There was a jar of hand crème in the drawer of the bedside stand. All my clothes were off and I had pulled the blankets from the bed. I snuggled down between the sheets nude.

This time it wasn't Elsbeth I pictured splayed out above me. It was Prince Radu Frumos Dracula of Wallachia-Transylvania. He was naked except for a black cape on his back. His hands held the cape out to the side like giant wings. His alabaster white skin glistened. Fangs emerged from his mouth. My lubricated right hand willed itself to my cock, my left to my balls.

Gazing at the prince, I filled he Kleenex with cum. God damn! I was in love. Holy shit! I was in love with a vampire.

CHAPTER THREE

KARL'S LOVE BITE

THE VOICE OF KARL TEPES

You know about how I introduced my buddy Tim Axelrod to Radu.

I want to tell you about how I got involved with the Nosferati myself.

You might not recognize me, but there's a better than even chance you've see me on the movie or TV screen. I'm not a star at all at Olympic Studios. My face is often very heavily made up in the parts I play. So people seeing me walking down the street seldom recognize me or ask me for an autograph.

I play tough guys and monsters and try to scare the Hell out of the audience. It's a great life, and I love it.

I want to start my story back when we were shooting that movie about the Jewish Mafia, *Kosher Nostra.* Did you see it? I was playing Sammy the Shiv, one of the more despicable hitmen in the gang.

Things weren't going too well with that scene where the

Don is pissed off because none of us hitmen could take out Hymie Moscowicz.

We shot the scene again and again and couldn't satisfy Perry White, the director.

At the end of the day I was feeling kind of down and discouraged. I didn't feel like going to any of the bars I frequent. I thought alcohol would serve more as a downer than otherwise. So I drove over to The Abbey on North Robertson in West Hollywood. Sometimes a coffee will perk me up.

I ordered myself a latte at the coffeehouse and sat myself down to check out the dudes who saunter into and out of the place. *That's* always an upper. Some of the best meat in Hollywood passes through those portals.

I was sipping my latte and feeling better and better as I scoped out the hunks.

Two guys walked in together. Not men I knew real well, but who were certainly acquaintances. They were Maurice Delatour and Rock Stone.

Maurice clapped a hand on my shoulder as they walked by and asked if they could join me.

I could use the company. And even if I'd really wanted to sit there alone, I wouldn't have been rude enough to tell them to get lost. So I assured them I would be delighted to have them as companions at my table.

They proceeded on to the bar to order their coffees.

You know Maurice Delatour, of course – the great French lover of the movies. His most recent flick, *Pepe le Suq*, was playing all over and was a financial and a critical success. It was the umpteenth remake of the old Jean Gabin movie *Pepe le Moko*. Maurice's co-star was Marlene Grabo. The two of them are long-time stars. A bit long in the tooth perhaps, but just right for the parts. Maurice and Marlene had been lovers back when they made *The Garden of Ali* and *Slave Girls of the Harem* a few years back. Having them back on the screen as mature lovers proved to be a winner. Maurice was always a good conversationalist and at Hollywood parties he and I had tossed down a few drinks together. I was happy to see him that evening.

His companion, Rock Stone, you probably don't know. He came to Hollywood in his teens or just barely out of them. A real stud muffin. He got a few male starlet roles in which he paraded about showing his sexy musculature and his nearly too-pretty face. His career was going exactly nowhere when he suddenly inherited a lot of dough from a rich uncle or something. He married Lacy Greeland, an older doll who had slept with most of the dignitaries in Hollywood.

Rock and Lacy began spending their newly acquired wealth as though there was no mañana. The parties they threw were the most lavish seen in Tinsel Town since the golden years. When they weren't throwing whingdings they were off on their yacht to Cabo or the Riviera.

It didn't take too long for the money to run out. Apparently Lacy had managed to siphon off enough cash into her own name to buy an interest in a company that makes horseshoes for racehorses or something like that.

Whatever it was, she is doing very nicely financially.

She and Rock divorced when the money he inherited ran out. She was now quite well-to-do and Rock was broke.

But a good-looking dude like Rock is never without friends. That evening he was paling around with Maurice Delatour. My guess was that Maurice was buying.

The two guys came back to the table and sat down with me. There was one odd thing about them. They were both wearing makeup. Not obvious cosmetics like the broads wear. Just a light paste to make them look slightly tan.

Hollywood guys in makeup aren't all that rare. But still…

We began talking about the great parties Rock had thrown. Rock was as stoked recalling them as Maurice and I were. To tell you the truth, that Rock dude really turned me on. Even though he was well past being the teenager starlet, he had a very healthy vigor and was still stunningly handsome. I kept thinking of what a thrill it would be to get him into bed.

We gabbed on and on. I finished my latte and went back for another.

What struck me as strange was that neither of my companions took even a sip of their drinks. Their coffee just turned cold and untasted in their cups.

I started back to the table with my second drink.

When I was walking back to the table I couldn't take my eyes off Rock.

What a gorgeous hunk of guy, with our without makeup on.

I settled down as close to Rock as I could manage without being gauche.

The conversation took a weird turn.

Maurice led off by saying, "Funny thing running into you here, Karl. Rock and I were just talking about you yesterday with a friend of ours."

That certainly surprised me. Some coincidence, huh?

"Really?" I responded. "That's funny. I don't remember my ears turning red yesterday."

We all laughed. Rock has beautiful teeth when he laughs. I basked in their gleam.

"No reason for them to turn red," Maurice told me. "It was all complimentary. This friend is a great fan of yours and said he'd like to meet you."

Fans are something I don't have many of. I began to wonder about this chance meeting at the coffeehouse.

"I could write my autograph on this paper napkin for him if that's what he'd like," I joked.

Laughter again and Rock's stunning smile.

"This friend of ours, he's a Romanian. Seems he heard you were Romanian, too," he claimed.

"No, Maurice," I said. "He's barking up the wrong tree there. I'm American. Born and raised here. My folks came from Romania, though. Our family name is Giurescu."

"I think that's what he meant," Rock said.

I loved the sound of his voice.

"You're of Romanian extraction," he continued. "You probably speak Romanian, and play Romanian vampires in your movies. All that intrigues our friend Radu."

Radu. Certainly a common enough Romanian name.

"He'd really like to meet you," Maurice said.

"Sure," I answered. "Any time."

I figured that should end the discussion.

But Rock pressed on.

"The guy's a nobleman. A prince," he said.

"An ex-prince, then," I clarified. "King Carol abdicated the throne of Romania in 1940 and his son Mihai became the last king of the country. My parents are ardent royalists. They named me after King Carol. But their hopes for Romania to ever become a monarchy again are just pipedreams. Romania hasn't had a prince for over fifty years."

"I suppose Prince Radu would enjoy discussing all this with you," Maurice said.

Rock seemingly had a great idea.

"Say, Maurice. You know that little party Radu's throwing tomorrow? The costume party?"

Maurice's face lit up.

"The prince would love for Karl to come. Are you free tomorrow night by any chance, Karl?"

This sounded like a blast. A party by a guy who claimed to be Prince of Romania. My folks would love it.

"Sure, I'm free," I said. "A costume party?"

"Yeah," Rock answered. "We're all coming in vampire costumes. Just your cup of tea, Karl. Come as one of those vampires you play so convincingly."

"Where's the party?" I asked, enthused.

"Mailamunte Castle," Rock said.

Mailamunte. Interesting. That's Romanian for "farther up the mountain." At least this so-called prince knew a little Romanian. I planned to talk to him in Romanian and see if he was the genuine article, at least linguistically.

They told me how to get to the castle. It turned out to really be "farther up the mountain."

The next evening, costumed in black suit and cape, whitened face, fangs – the whole nine yards – I followed the directions they gave me. I found myself being welcomed at a castle that looked suspiciously like the set for the old Bela Lugosi Dracula movie.

I was welcomed by a man with a disjointed neck. He was well made up like a Hollywood movie vampire with white greasepaint on cheeks and forehead and deep black circles about the eyes. His hair came to a widow's peak and was slicked back vampire style. I wondered at the time if the offset head and neck were part of the act. It gave me quite a jolt.

I later discovered that Clement had been hanged and had a permanent disfigurement. Tim has already covered his situation in Appendix IV, page 129.

"Welcome to our home," he said. "Enter of your own free will. I am Clement the major domo."

In my full vampire outfit I entered Mailamunte Castle.

The castle exterior, as I mentioned, was 1930s Gothic. Inside, though, I stepped into a perfectly modern, beautifully decorated livingroom.

Livingroom doesn't quite describe the size. For the room is as large as a grand ballroom. But the tables, chairs, wall decorations, lighting, et cetera, were contemporary, comfortable and in perfect taste.

I took a quick look around at the crowd. There appeared to be ten or eleven of them, all in whiteface, black makeup, capes, the vampire drill Rock and Maurice had promised. I could recognize some of them behind their makeup. Rock and Maurice, of course. Marlene Grabo was there. Her distinctive cheekbones gave her away immediately. I thought I recognized the cowboy actor Tex McCall from his height and bow legs.

I didn't have time to try to recognize any others because Rock Stone was approaching me. How that man could walk! Grace personified.

And, I must say, the dude looked *great* in a cape.

"Karl!" he saluted me with enthusiasm. "Just in time for the party."

He put his arm round my waist to conduct me to a young man who was in the center of the crowd.

"Come over here," Rock said as he led me. "I'd like you to meet our host."

The young man we were heading for separated himself from the crowd and approached me. I figured him to be in his young twenties at the most. But sometimes it's hard to tell behind the greasepaint.

When we were face to face with the young man, Rock introduced us.

"Your Highness," he said. "Allow me to introduce the great character actor Karl Tepes. Karl, His Highness Prince Radu Frumos Dracula."

The "prince" extended his hand, which I shook.

Dracula? I'm thinking. *Now I* know *this is a put on.*

"Buna seara, Domnul Giurescu," he said with a charming smile. "Bun-venit."

'Multumese," I replied.

"I am afraid most of my guests do not speak our language," he said. "Might we converse in English?"

"Of course," I answered.

"Ladies and gentlemen," the prince announced. "Our guest of honor, the noted actor, Karl Tepes."

Everyone applauded. I was truly surprised.

"Everyone present is well acquainted with your work," the prince said. "I have collected copies of every vampire movie ever made, back to the silent films of 1896, 1901, and 1922. We show the films here regularly at the castle and everyone is always impressed by your portrayals.

"So I asked our good friends Maurice and Rock to contact you and invite you here so we could meet you. I hope you are not offended at this surprise party."

So Maurice and Rock *had* stalked me to The Abbey. It was no chance meeting. Their friend wanted to throw a surprise party for me.

"Offended?' Not at all," I responded. "I am honored, Your Majesty,"

"No more of 'Your Majesty.'" he smiled. "If I may call you Karl, or your Romanian name Carol, I would like you to call me Radu."

We agreed on Karl and Radu.

He said we could talk about the politics of his princely title at another time.

Clement had left the room, but he came back with an ice bucket. In the bucket was a bottle of wine and some champagne flutes.

He was followed by a tiny Blackamoor lady in a turban who was bearing a tray of tiny liqueur glasses containing a deep red liquid.

"Would you care for a glass of champagne?" Radu asked me.

I said yes.

The Blackamoor took the tray to some of the guests.

Clement poured champagne for me and four other guests. I and the other champagne folks were not even offered the red stuff.

Drugs? I wondered.

We all had either champagne in hand or what I decided to call Redeye.

Radu proposed a flowery toast to me. When he had laid it on to the point of embarrassing me, he said "Felicitari!"

Everyone repeated the word, probably the only word in Romanian most of them knew.

I answered "Mutulmesc foart mult." And that was as much Romanian as I spoke for the rest of the evening.

"Come," Radu addressed the crowd. "We have a musical treat in store. Countess Ioana has agreed to favor us with music."

An appreciative sound arose from the crowd. The countess was clearly a favorite.

Radu presented an arm to a very lovely young lady. I sensed that the two were lovers. Perhaps even married to each other? I thought not. I surmised, correctly, that the young lady was Countess Ioana.

The two led the crowd out of the great hall, down a wide corridor, and into what turned out to be the music room. There were chairs arranged to face a piano, a harpsichord, and a collection of stringed and percussion instruments.

Radu led the lady to the front, bowed gallantly to her, and took a seat in the front row.

Rock and Maurice had accompanied me to the room, Rock's arm

resting lightly on my shoulder. Pleasure radiated through my body at his touch. The three of us sat in the second row. The others sat scattered about the room.

Countess Ioana (who I somehow doubted at the time was any more of a countess than Radu was a prince or a Dracula) went to the displayed instruments and picked up a cobza.

I knew the instrument because my folks had dragged me to Romanian folk festivals when I was young. The cobza is a short-necked, unfretted lute-like instrument.

The countess sat in a chair facing us, tuned the instrument, and began to sing.

She had a preternaturally beautiful soprano voice. The song she sang took me back to my youth. I did not know whether I had heard this particular song before. If I had, I knew that it had not been sung so beautifully. She sang it in Romanian. I have made an attempt to render it in English.

Ionana sang:
I never told the wind how well I loved him,
And yet I loved him well.
The long spring evenings will return,
Then will the meadows tell the blossoms
"Here you are again."

And no one knows how much I weep
In this, my empty house.
No one can know, for empty is my house.
I used to sing of how my love
Said to me once, once long ago,
"Oh, never sing that song!
"For it will do me harm in fortune's eyes."
And then, my love, he went away.
I only thought of him.
And so I sang again my song.

A man came to my door.

This man was a wanderer
And thus I spoke to him:
"Oh you who come from far away
"And farther more shall go
"Where is my love, my heart's delight.
"Please tell me if you know."
The stranger bore a blood-stained knife
And yet I did not fear.
Then said that stranger unto me
"Sing now that song to me
"And I will tell you everything
"That has befallen him."

So I forgot my true love's words
And sang the song again.

I saw the wanderer trembling then,
His face was pale and wan.
"I am your love. I have returned
"In form Undead forever.
"And since you sang the song you sang
"You shall accursed be."
And now and e're my fate shall be
To hear that song, eternally.

I never told the wind how well I loved him,
And yet I loved him well.
The long spring evenings will return,
Then will the meadows tell the blossoms
"Here you are, again."

When the song was finished, I found that I was weeping. The rendition had been incredibly moving. Hearing the poetry of the folksong, sung softly in my mother's tongue, caused me to get emotional. And, also, I had consumed a fair amount of Radu's champagne by then.

The applause was heartfelt. She sang two more songs for us.

(One of those songs, in translation to English, will be found in Appendix VI on page 133 for those with a further taste for Romanian folksongs.)

When she finished, Radu arose, took the cobza from her, kissed her hand, returned the instrument to its place on the stand, and walked her to the chair next to where he had been sitting.

When she was seated, he gallantly thanked her, than addressed the party.

"Fellow revelers," he announced. "In honor of our guest, Mister Tepes, we are showing one of his movies in the theater room. Because this is such a happy occasion, we are projecting the comedy in which he elicits so much delightful laughter from his audience. The film is *Fangs a Lot*."

A murmur of approval swept through the crowd.

As we all stood to go to the castle's movie theater, Radu took his leave from the countess and came over to Rock, Maurice, and me. He addressed me directly.

"As my guest, I want you to know you have a choice as to the entertainment you favor at this time. We can go enjoy the cinema. Or, if you prefer, the four of us can go to the library and chat."

The choice was a no brainer for me. I did not need to see *Fangs a Lot* again, ever. But the opportunity to converse with this stunningly handsome man who claimed not only to be a prince, but a Dracula was too much to refuse.

And to enhance the decision, to have Rock Stone at my side during the conversation…irresistible.

Radu led us through a labyrinth of wide corridors to his library. It was furnished like an English baronial library with comfortable overstuffed leather chairs, oak tables, a fireplace, and, most impressive of all, floor to ceiling bookshelves filled with tomes. I am not much of a reader, and, even so, I was impressed. I thought of my friend Tim, who is somewhat of a scholar, and how he would relish this room, losing himself in the lore that must reside within all those book covers.

I was surprised that there was a fire blazing in the hearth. How did they know anyone would be coming to this room? Who would have known?

The chairs were arranged in a conversational group around a round oaken table. There was a decanter with some brandy snifters on the table along with a humidor of cigars, some ashtrays, and matches.

Radu asked if I would care for any cognac or a cigar. I declined. It was clear that none of my companions were inclined to smoke, sniff, or swallow.

In that environment it was very easy to relax into comfortable conversation.

"Shall we remove our cosmetics, Gentlemen?" Radu asked. "I feel they lend a bizarre air to a group of friends engaging in conversation."

I and the others agreed. But I couldn't see how we were going to manage to take off our greasepaint in that venue.

Radu clapped twice, and in through a side door came two servants wheeling a table. They were followed by two others in the same livery. On the table were the cloths, tissues, and crèmes every actor is so familiar with.

"Let us rest our heads on the backs of the chairs and the servants will restore us to our everyday faces," Radu said.

We complied and the four servants performed as professionally as the makeup artists at the studio. When they finished their job of removing our greasepaint, they marched out of the library wheeling their table with them.

With their cosmetics removed, my three companions appeared strikingly pale in the reflection of the blaze in the fireplace. I understood why Rock and Maurice had been wearing makeup at The Abbey. They were uncommonly pale for people living in Southern California. Rock's skin was alabaster pale. And Radu appeared even paler than Rock.

"I assume," Radu said to me, "that you may have some questions about who I really am. Let me begin by re-stating that I have been an admirer of your cinematic depictions for a long time. I hope you will not be offended when I tell you that I took the liberty of assembling a body of information about you."

I was surprised, but not offended. I suppose I was even somewhat flattered.

He continued.

"I was delighted to discover that you, one of my favorite actors, are of Romanian stock, like me. Your parents, the Giurescus, I know to be of Royalist persuasion. You therefore were early made aware that Romania has not had a prince since Kings Carol and Mihai in the 1940s."

I acknowledged that was the case and that I had wondered about his title.

"At one time," he continued, "I was a prince of Wallachia and Transylvania. The title tends to cling despite political vicissitudes."

I know that titles do "stick." But there had not been a prince of those Romanian provinces for ages. Centuries even. And my host looked to be younger even than my friend Tim.

I was sure my skepticism showed on my face.

"I believe I know what you are thinking, My Friend," he told me. "You have steeped yourself professionally in portrayals of the Undead. Do you believe that we are merely fabrications of myth and folklore?"

"We?!" What the fuck did he mean by 'we'? Was this kid trying to tell me he was a goddam vampire? Or, even more, that those other two guys were Undead too? It seemed the practical joke on me was beginning to unwind.

I can take a joke as well as the next guy. Well, okay. I was willing to play along with the gag. I found it pretty damned entertaining. It really was turning out to be a night to remember.

"You're telling me, Radu, that you really are a vampire?"

"Actually, we prefer the term Nosferatu," he said with a pleasant smile.

"A more genteel word, of course," I agreed. "You are telling me you were a Nosferatu prince of Transylvania?"

"I know that is hard to believe. But that is what I am telling you," he answered.

I looked at Rock and Maurice.

"And how about you guys? Are you going to tell me you two have somehow become Nosferati as well?"

They nodded their heads and smiled.

"All right, I buy it," I lied. "Tell me about it. But I believe I *will* have a bit of that cognac and a cigar after all."

Radu poured me a drink. Maurice lit my cigar. And Rock pushed an ashtray in my direction.

I took a swig of the cognac. Rock lit my cigar.

And I settled in to listen to what I thought, at first, was their bullshit.

Radu gave me a very short version of the story he told Tim weeks later at the Transibar in West Hollywood. I didn't know too much about Transylvanian history. But I pretty much bought the historical stuff he was telling about anyway. What I really had to doubt was that this dude was born in 1438 and was the brother of the Dracula depicted, luridly, in print and film.

Still, I was fairly flush with the champagne I'd drunk in the Great Hall, the brandy I was sniffing, and drinking at the moment. And the heady effects of the excellent Corona Corona I was smoking.

I wanted to buy the unlikely story. But, come on, Man. Sitting there listening to a five or six hundred year old vampire prince from Transylvania? In the company of guys I knew, who claimed to be vampires too? Oh, *excuse* me. Nosferati? Harder to swallow than the smooth cognac.

"How about the other guests in that theater room watching the movie?" I asked.

He told me some were Nosferati and some were Voevods. The ones who were Nosferati could be distinguished in that they did not partake of the champagne.

"What *were* the Nosferati drinking?" I was curious but almost afraid to ask.

"Blood," he replied coolly.

That was what I was afraid he was gonna say. And also what I hoped he'd say.

He explained that the Nosferati can only drink wine from the bloodstream of a mortal or of a Voevod. I involuntarily felt my own neck.

We all chuckled a bit.

"You need not worry," Radu said. "No one receives the Nosferatu

Kiss unless he or she requests it. We do not, and never have, preyed on mortal beings."

Well! *That* was a relief.

I understood the concept of Voevods. In Romanian it meant something like "privileged people" or "insiders." These had to be people who received what Radu called the Nosferatu Kiss, but who were not turned into Nosferati by the experience.

Maurice stepped in and explained how Voevods become Nosferati through the infusion of purakh. I think you already know all about that.

"All of you, those in this room and in the theater room," I asked. "Why did you all agree to become Voevods in the first place?"

"For most of us," Rock said. "It's the sex."

Now *that* dude had caught my interest.

"Tell me about the sex," I asked.

"There's nothing like it," he said. "For men Voevods the orgasms when you are being fanged go on and on. It's not a case of come, wait, come, wait. It's come-come-come. And the heightened sensations are otherworldly. Before I became a Voevod, I thought I had experienced every sexual experience imaginable. But wow! And for the women, the heightened sexual experience is equally vibrant."

The dude had me turned on. Whether all this was a giant hoax or not, I was hoping I could get this stud into bed and let him fang me and bang me. I was going to play this to the hilt. Otherworldly or not, I wanted sex with that hunk.

Maurice had a word to say.

"You may wonder why those of us who graduated beyond the Voevod state decided to do so."

I hadn't really wondered. My mind was on other matters. But since he'd brought the subject up…

"Most of us want to retain whatever youth we have," he answered himself. "You observe Prince Radu. He maintains the youth, the looks, the vigor, and the sexual potency he had when he became transfigured ages ago. Our friend Rock here chose this path at a later age than Radu, but he became not only immortal but will always have the body and virility of a man in his mid-twenties. I became Undead at a much later age, but chose to never become older.

"In exchange, we gave up all daytime activities. We are lifeless in our caskets from sunrise to sunset. But... Oh the nightlife!"

I thought that I probably would never want to give up my mortality. I enjoyed being free to do my thing come daylight or starlight. But sex with Rock as a Nosferatu and me as a Voevod. *That* was something I could dig. So, I bought their whole fucking unlikely story.

Radu delved somewhat personally into my mind. Or more likely, he was reading my aura. I wasn't hip to the aura jive at the time. I didn't learn about that until Tim and I met Radu at the Transibar. Even then, I didn't quite get it. And to tell the truth, I still don't quite know what the aura bit is. And what's more, I hardly give damn.

But what Radu was picking up was that I had the hots for Rock and was probably willing to risk a lot to get beneath the sheets with him.

Radu came out with it.

"I detect, Friend Karl, that you are attracted to Rock Stone. If it is not too personal, tell me if that is so or not."

I'm hardly the blushing kind. But having it brought out in the open so abruptly caught me by surprise. I could feel the blood rush to my face.

For some reason, I couldn't look Radu in the face. And what's more, I couldn't bring myself to steal a glance at Rock to see how he was taking Radu's question.

I felt like a goddam kid caught with a libidinous thought. It had been years since I'd been embarrassed by anything. Being a transvestite in Hollywood has a way of making you feel shameless. But I recognized the old feelings of being "found out" that went back to my teen years.

I managed to squeeze out an answer. I'm not real sure today just what the words were. But they managed to express that I found Rock sexually attractive.

Radu answered.

"You may not have noticed, but Rock holds similarly favorable views concerning you."

So there it was. I knew the moment of truth had arrived. I was a mortal, sitting in a room of a castle atop a hill, surrounded by vampires. I had been assured that I was safe from their bite unless I asked for it.

The chances were that I could get fucked by the gorgeous hunk of stuff sitting across from me if I could bring myself to ask him to sink his fangs into me and drink my blood. What would my decision be?

I'll tell you right off the bat. The decision did not come from my brains. It came directly from my balls. The words were formed on my lips prompted by testosterone.

I looked directly at Rock. His eyes met mine. He smiled invitingly. God, what beautiful teeth the dude had.

"Rock," I said. "I would be honored if you would favor me with the Nosferatu Kiss."

There! It was out. My brain was amazed at what my nuts had made me say. But it was said. And my body (if not my brain) was glad.

Rock answered me in what I perceived to be dulcet and caring tones.

"I would be happy to respond to your request, Karl. But I want to be sure that you know exactly what you're asking. The experience of becoming a Voevod is not to be taken lightly. You are aware that I have not tried in the least to seduce you into that state, aren't you?"

I agreed verbally that such was the case. But deep down I knew that was not really true. I *had* been seduced by the guy. His gorgeous masculinity had swept me off my feet. His buddy, the prince, had pretty much told me the conditions under which I could bed Rock.

But whether I had been seduced or not, bedding the hunk was what I wanted more than anything in the world. Having his sexy white fangs penetrate my bloodstream would be a new extreme in my sexual adventures. A welcome one.

My answer was yes, yes, yes.

Without a further word, both Rock and I stood up. My desire for him showed at my crotch.

He held out his hand to me. I walked around the table, took his hand, and let him lead me wherever he willed.

Without taking leave of my host or Maurice, I accompanied Rock, hand in hand, out the library door and into the wide corridor.

Once in the corridor, he put his arm around my waist. Good Lord! Even if things went no further than this, I was in Heaven.

It seemed as though we walked the hallways for hours. It was probably more like minutes, but I had lost all sense of time.

At length we came to a door that I hoped would lead to a bedroom rather than to a coffin. But, if it should turn out to be sex in a coffin, I could deal with that, too.

He opened the door, and I was pleased to see that the room was furnished with a bed rather than a coffin. Beds are normal. Coffins are kinky. Things were kinky enough. So I was happy to see the goddam bed.

I had to break our silence.

"What now?" I asked.

After all, I had never before had sex with a vampire…Oops, a Nosferatu.

"Let's just get comfortable with each other," Rock smiled. "Why don't we get out of these cumbersome duds and just lie down and relax with each other?"

Sounded good to me.

We watched each other undress. I remembered seeing him in those movies he'd made as the number two juvenile in the cast. I remembered ogling him in his parts as he strutted his stuff and flexed his muscles. I think he may have given me a hardon even then. Seeing him disrobe in this bedroom was enough to give me a real woodie. His cock was flaccid as he undressed. But what a gorgeous cock it was, hard, soft, or in between.

He turned down the blankets and stretched out on the sheets. I lay down next to him and stared at the ceiling.

I was in no rush. I wanted to savor every moment. I lay perfectly still. It seemed to be understood that Rock would originate and orchestrate the rest of the evening.

And that was exactly as I wanted it to be.

I lay there next to him, my left hip grazing his right. I was in no hurry, and neither was he. I was happy just to be there by his side.

At length, his right hand brushed against my thigh. I hesitated, then slid my left hand onto his. The touches were butterfly soft. My excitement mounted. I am not sure whether music was piped into the room. I heard music, but it may have all been internal.

His fingers slid around to my left inner thigh. I couldn't help giving a start. A start of delight and pleasure that I simply could not suppress. When I allowed my hand to softly caress his inner thigh, I thought I heard him sigh. The love music played on. I truly am not sure whether it came over the airways or was purely a product of my own inner joy and contentment.

We continued to lie there perfectly still, with only our hands and fingers in motion. I was breathing very deeply. I felt that he was too. But the joyful turmoil within me prevented me from really knowing.

One of his fingers just barely grazed the bottom of my scrotum. I was afraid I would come on the spot.

I did not come, but the palpitations at my peckerhead were intense. I found the same spot on him, just a bit above his perineum.

When he encircled my balls in a soft fondle, I thought I was done for. But by some force of will I kept from erupting. I gently fondled his balls in response. We both sighed.

We simultaneously took hold of each other's cock. I took a loving look at his face.

His eyeteeth had lengthened and sharpened. His fangs had emerged from their retraction. Those fangs entranced me. As wonderful as his cock felt in my hand, I knew the feel of those fangs on my neck would be more thrilling still.

He let loose of my prick. I released his as well. I turned on my side facing away from him. He brought his body next to mine, spoon fashion. That enticing rock-hard prick of his rested against my asscrack.

He raised his head and hovered over me. His sweet breath assailed my nostrils. I tensed, but with loving anticipation.

He lowered his mouth to my neck. The moment was coming.

I thought, "This is the moment I have waited for all my life."

Those sharp fangs rested lightly on my skin.

"Are you sure this is what you want?" he whispered.

"Yes, yes, yes," I breathed.

The sharp pang I felt as his fangs penetrated to my jugular were offset by the most exquisite physical experience I had ever known.

His penis entered my asshole as he began to suck my blood through his fangs. I was being fanged. I was being fucked by a vampire.

I was delirious.

The rapture I felt that whole evening, up through the early hours of the morning, were indescribable. I know I must have lost about a pint of blood as it was sipped lovingly from my veins. It was my gift to my phantom lover. He drew sustenance from me. I drew ecstasy from him.

When I left the castle around four in the morning, I did not feel I was the same person who had entered it the previous night.

I was a Voevod. A Voevod saturated with love.

CHAPTER FOUR

VAMP

THE VOICE OF ROB ROBERTS

I'm Rob Roberts. You've probably seen some of the movies I've written, produced, and directed. In other words, I'm what we folks in Hollywood call an *auteur.*

I auteured something I called a tetralogy a while back. That was a pretentious name for four pictures produced with a common theme.

It sounded like a good idea at the time. The sequence followed a cowboy and a strongman goon through four venues.

The first picture was a success with the crowds. They loved it. The critics hated it. The second one got a pretty good response from the moviegoers. It was razzed even more than the first one by the critics.

I produced parts three and four, and the critics got pretty vicious.

And my fan base dribbled down to just about zilch.

I had thought the tetralogy was a good idea. Turned out, it laid an egg.

So I lost my audience. I lost my backers. And I lost my money.

And, worst of all, I lost my wife, Willa.

But I didn't lose Willa because of my tetralogy. She had panned it from the beginning. But that had nothing to do with our split-up.

I lost her because she had an affair with Maurice Delatour. You know him. The movies' so-called "Great French Lover."

When I caught the two of them red-handed in their lovenest, I guess I had a kind of hissy-fit. I divorced Willa. Maurice's wife divorced him. Willa and Maurice got married. And, as I understood it, lived unhappily ever after.

I regretted my prudish response to Willa's fling about as soon as the divorce papers cooled off. Sure, she had been unfaithful. One friggin' time. This is Hollywood. And I'd kind of dared her to do it. I had been a fool. And I regretted it.

Imagine my surprise when Willa showed up at my apartment door in Larchmont Towers a couple of years after our break-up. It was about seven in the evening. No telephone call ahead of time.

The doorbell rang. I answered it.

"Hi, Rob," she said. "I just dropped by on the off-chance you might be home. Did I catch you at a bad time?"

"Come in, Willa," I said. "I'm really happy to see you."

She entered and looked around my livingroom with curiosity.

"Can I offer you anything?" I asked. "Coffee, tea, gin, me?"

It was a lame joke, but she laughed.

'Nothing, really," she answered. "I'm not really thirsty."

"Then have a seat," I invited.

She took one of the guest chairs. I settled into my rocker.

"Gee, Willa," I said truthfully. "I'm really glad you dropped by. This is gonna sound corny, I know. But I've gotta tell you. I've really missed seeing you."

"We had some great times together," she answered. "I've missed you too. If I hadn't gone off on that silly affair with Maurice, the good times would've continued, wouldn't they?"

"I was more at fault than I was willing to admit even to myself," I replied. "I said some pretty dumb things that pushed you into it. And afterward, I responded to what you did like a prig and a bastard."

"How do you spell 'prig'?" she asked.

"That's easy," I replied. "P-R-I-C-K"

We laughed and I felt the air had cleared. Here we were, Willa and Rob, sitting cozily and conversing freely and enjoyably.

In my loneliness from her, I had assumed we could never be friends again. Sitting with her in the comfort of my livingroom, I asked myself the question: Can I ever again become even friends with this woman I loved, married, and divorced? I listened to my heart and the answer came back a resounding "yes."

"You were right about my tetralogy," I said.

Willa smiled wistfully, remembering what she had said about it.

"I suppose I was cruel in revealing my feelings about a work you were so passionately involved in."

"It isn't cruel to be honest," I replied.

"Oh, it can be," she averred. "I know people who take pleasure in hurting others' feelings and excusing themselves by claiming they were only being honest. Honesty can hurt. Hurt needlessly."

I agreed with her that such can be the case. But told her I didn't think her views on my tetralogy fell into that basket.

"You see, My Dear," I explained. "You were right about my attempt at cinematic grandeur. You saw through the concept, and, like a good wife, told me it was a crock."

"Crock?" she laughed. "Was I really that crude"

"No, Willa. I'm just scrambling for words. The critics were right from the beginning. The movie-going public began to agree with them as I kept cranking out the crap. You were on the right side from the beginning."

"Does it hurt?" she asked sympathetically.

I didn't have to think over the answer.

"In that period of time, I lost my backers, I lost my public, I lost my money, I lost my self-confidence, and most of all, I lost you.

"Willa, you ask if it hurts. It hurt then. And it still hurts."

I would have loved for her to get up, come over to me, and

give me a hug and a kiss. She did not. And we both knew she should not. The significance of such a move would have been enveloped in sentimentality. This was not a moment for sentimentality.

"Enough of this wallowing in 'poor me' talk," I said. "I produced a bomb. In the business I'm in, it's a risk. Creativity doesn't guarantee anyone anything. Life goes on."

I couldn't think of any more platitudes and let myself look at this woman whom I had loved and realized I still did.

She was so pale. Had she kept herself in a dark room ever since we parted? It is not easy to be so pale living under the Southern California sun. The term "deathly pale" occurred to me. Had she been ill? Was she ill at the moment?

Yet, other than the pallor, she appeared hearty enough. It would be too "honest" to blurt out something like, "You look awfully pale, Dear. Are you dying of cancer or something?" I smiled at the crude thought.

"Something's amusing you," Willa said.

"Just an inward chuckle at the string of clichés I was blurting out at you. Tell me. Are you still living in Hollywood? I haven't heard a word about you since our divorce was final. Do you and Maurice still live at The Emperor's Arms?"

She laughed.

"No, no. We sold the place to a rich gentleman from Arizona who keeps it well managed as part of his holdings. Maurice and I have moved to a kind of commune up in the Hollywood Hills."

I was aghast.

"You two joined a cult?" I asked.

"I guess it does sound like that," she said. "It's a lifestyle we were attracted to and we decided to become a part of it."

I'll have to admit I didn't like the sound of it. But as an ex-husband, I didn't think I had any right to object or even show much apprehension.

"We live very nicely. As a matter of fact, we live in a castle that was built years ago up above Mulholland Drive. The owner of the castle is a very wealthy businessman. He's even interested in investing in a movie project."

I was interested.

"Not the sort of film you'd probably be interested in, though, Rob."

"What kind of movie *is* he interested in financing?" I asked.

"He wants to do a vampire movie."

I had never been big on the genre. Not my kind of thing at all.

"You're right," I said. "He should contact Otto Caruthers. He's been very successful in the horror film line. I'd be happy to get this businessman friend of yours in contact with Otto if he'd like."

"He'd probably appreciate that," she said. "Tell you what. Why don't you come up to the castle Friday night? Are you free?"

I said I was.

"Radu, who's the head honcho of the community, runs movies for the group every Friday night. He's nuts about vampire movies. He has everything from the old German silent film made in the 1920s, *Nosferatu*, to Otto's last vampire comedy *Fangs a Lot*. It's lots of fun

"I know you're not real big on those kinds of movies, but they're enjoyable to see in a crowd.

"And there are quite a few people you know in our community. Would you believe Tex has joined our group?"

Tex McCall. He was the star in my tetralogy. Small world. It *would* be good to see him again.

"And you could talk to Radu about your contacts with Otto. It would be great fun."

She had intrigued me. Seeing some of the old vampire movies even had a kind of kinky attraction. Add to that a reunion with people I'd known and worked with.

I told her I'd be happy to go up to her place to see movies and old friends.

She told me how to get there. I've driven those hills enough to know I'd have no problem following her instructions.

She got up to leave. I yearned to kiss her. But I knew that would be a big mistake. She was no longer mine.

At the door, we looked in each other's eyes, smiled, and shook hands.

And my Willa disappeared into the night.

All the next day visions of Willa filled my mind. I felt surges of regret that my puritanical urgings had driven her out of my life. I was anxious about what kind of cult she might have let herself get sucked into in that so-called castle atop the hills. There were sweet longings as I realized that I would be with her Friday. I felt that just being with her would begin to heal my self-inflicted heart wounds.

At six-thirty on Friday I was in my '67 Corvette chugging up the hills. Somehow, I had never driven to Summit Drive before. But I knew where it was and how to get there.

Where the road stopped, there was a gate. And beyond the gate, a narrow one-lane paved path led up the hill. On the gate, as Willa had told me, was a simple brass plate with the image of a dragon embossed on it. Next to the plate was a callbox.

I pressed the button on the callbox and was answered. I gave the password and my name. That was enough to swing the gate back.

I drove in and up the hill to the top.

People in Hollywood are not unacquainted with the fact that there's an old castle-like structure up in the hills. There are enough eccentric buildings constructed by Hollywood zanies to fill a book. I had never been very curious about any of them. And I had never known anyone else who gave a damn about them either.

When I pulled into the plaza in front of the place I stood next to my car for a while and took it all in. I felt I had seen this place before somewhere. In a movie, probably. I thought perhaps they had shot one of the old black-and-white horror movies up here. Maybe even had built the place as an elaborate and very expensive set.

So *this* was where Willa was living now. In some kind of goddam commune or sect. I hoped to Hell she knew what she was doing.

Oh, well, Rob. Stop stewing and just go ring the doorbell.

The portals were enormous, and somewhat intimidating. I pulled a chain, waited only a matter of seconds, and the door swung open.

I was greeted by a character right out of those nineteen thirties horror movies. It looked like his neck had been broken and reset crooked so his head was leaning off to one side. He greeted me in a friendly enough fashion.

He said, "Welcome to our home. Enter of your own free will. I am Clement the major domo."

You don't run into a major domo every day, do you? Especially one with a broken neck. And what was that "enter of your own free will" business all about? I had stirrings of concern about what Willa had gotten herself into.

Willa was expecting me, of course. I had barely entered a large hall when she came over to me, gave me a friendly hug, and welcomed me.

"I'm so glad you could come," she said. "Several of your old friends and acquaintances are here, and are anxious to see you."

I looked around, and sure enough, there they were smiling at me.

They gathered around, shook my hand, slapped my back, and gave me pecks on the cheek. Some I knew very well. Some were part of the Hollywood crowd that were merely acquaintances. I had become rather reclusive after my last flop and was happy to see them all again.

Maurice Delatour was there, naturally. When I had last seen him, I knew him as the guy who had seduced my wife. All that was now water flushed down the toilet. I had no hard feelings as I shook his hand.

There was Marlene Grabo. She was a true Hollywood legend and had made a great comeback in a movie staring her and Maurice. I hadn't seen the flick but I knew all about what a financial success it was. She favored me with a peck on both cheeks.

Tex McCall came sauntering over. Tall, thin, nearly gaunt, ruggedly handsome. He'd been the leading man in my last four disastrous movies. He'd gone on afterward to make a successful Western set in Deadwood. I hadn't seen it. But I was happy I hadn't ruined his career.

Rock Stone was there. I didn't know him well, but had been invited to his lavish parties. I had only attended one of his bashes but I remembered him.

There were others of the Hollywood crowd. All of them looking well. Except for one thing. I wondered why they were all so pale. Pale in the way Willa was. I wondered if it was the lights. But no. Willa had that same pale, nearly luminous complexion, back at my place in Larchmont

Towers the previous evening. Did all the members of this commune have some weird reason to avoid getting out into the California sunshine? A mystery.

A handsome young man, well dressed, sporting a cape, and wearing a stickpin featuring a stunning diamond, came up to me after all the greetings were completed.

Willa introduced me.

"Radu," she said. "I would like you to meet Rob Roberts."

"How do you do," he said with one of the warmest smiles I had ever seen.

"Thank you for allowing me to come to your place," I said.

"I am delighted you could come," he replied. "I am acquainted with your work and admire it very much."

I wondered if that was true. If so, maybe he was the last person on earth who was still a fan.

Then I chastised myself.

Stop being such a crybaby, Rob. Stop feeling sorry for yourself and accept the compliment.

"Thank you," was what I said, and all I had to say.

"Did Willa tell you of my cinematic eccentricity?" he asked. "I am inordinately fond of vampire movies. Every Friday evening we project a different one in our theater room. Tonight we are showing Carl Dreyer's 1932 French language masterpiece, *Vampyr*. There are English sub-titles, of course. Do you know the film?"

I didn't and said so.

"I think you, of all people, will appreciate Dreyer's artistry. It is like watching a moving Seurat painting. Quite extraordinary."

"I look forward to seeing it," I said.

And, to tell the truth, I meant it.

Here was a guy who said he liked my work. And in describing this old French flick, he sounded like a man who knew his stuff.

We were joined by a gorgeous young lady who was introduced to me as Countess Ioana. Like the others, she had that pale luminosity. But, if possible, even more so. Drop-dead exquisite complexion. A countess, eh? Well, she was the best looking countess I could ever have imagined.

Radu and the countess led the way out of the Great Hall. The rest of us followed. Willa took my arm, and thus joined we proceeded with the others down a series of hallways to the theater room. It was not unlike the screeningroom down at Olympic. But somewhat more comfortable.

We took our seats, the lights dimmed, and the film began to roll.

I was blown out of my mind by Dreyer's film. Regardless of genre, it was a masterpiece. The pointillism of the camerawork was pure magic. The writing was subtle rather than garish. The horror was all suggested, never portrayed. A true auteur was clearly behind the writing, the producing, and the directing.

I knew that there had been over ninety vampire films produced in languages ranging from Turkish and Hindi to German and French. Most of them were horror exploitation flicks But having seen this one film, I knew I would never dismiss a genre simply because of esthetic prejudices.

(For more information on Dreyer's film, see Appendix V, page 131.)

When the show was over, Willa asked me if I would like to get together with Radu. The previous evening, I had told her that I could probably help him in his endeavor to finance a movie. I had even suggested getting him together with Otto Caruthers. But I was now hesitant about mentioning Otto to him. After seeing Dreyer's work, I felt Caruthers' vampire pictures were schlock.

However, if this Radu person wanted to talk movie business, I was game. And besides, I knew Willa really wanted me to.

I told her if she could arrange a date, a time, and a place for Radu and me to get together, I would probably be able to make it.

"How about now?" she asked.

I had nothing better to do.

"Sure," I said. "If you will be there with me."

Additional time with Willa would be a major plus.

As Radu and his squeeze Ionna walked by, Radu stopped for a moment to smile at us.

"Rob says he could talk with you now if you'd like," she said.

I could tell he was not surprised. It seemed clear that they had planned just such an occasion for this time.

"Fine," he said. "Why don't the two of you go down to the library. I need to see Clement for just a minute first. Then I'll be right there."

Willa led me through the hallways to the room that was obviously the library. It was a room full of well-stocked bookshelves.

Willa and I sat on a couple of the comfortable chairs ranged around a table. There was a decanter on the table and a few brandy snifters.

"Care for a brandy while we're waiting?" she asked. "It's Courvoisier VSOP."

Seeing the film and being with her were heady enough.

"No thanks," I answered. "Go ahead and have some if you want."

She didn't want any either.

We only had to wait a few minutes for Radu to enter.

"Sorry to keep you waiting," he said as he seated himself.

"No problem," I answered. "I was enjoying sitting here looking around at your library. Quite a collection of books."

"I have enjoyed collecting rare books for a long time," he said. "After our discussion, please feel free to browse."

I thanked him, knowing that I would not take him up on his offer. Rare books were hardly my thing.

"Did you enjoy the cinema?" he asked.

I told him how it had affected me esthetically and emotionally. And that it had radically changed my view of the genre.

He laughed politely.

"It *is* an astounding piece of work, isn't it?" he replied. "There are many dreadful vampire movies. Even the most exploitive of them, though, amuse me and many others of our kind."

His *kind*? What was *that* supposed to mean? I didn't ask.

"Willa tells me *you* are interested in investing in a film yourself," I broached.

"Yes," he answered. "That is true. And I must admit that I was devious enough to ask her to invite you to our castle so we could discuss it."

"If it was devious," I halfway joked, "I hope you will continue in that vein. I was delighted to see Willa again. You did me a favor on that account. I have very much enjoyed your hospitality. And I was delighted with the projection of Dreyer's masterpiece."

Radu seemed pleased with my response.

"I have wanted to help finance a film along the lines of my longtime interest," he told me. "A film about the Nosferati, as we prefer to call vampires."

Who's this "we"? I wondered. I wished Willa had told me more about this guy. Well, why not ask?

"'We' being exactly who?" I queried.

"I am a businessman," he replied. "I have several business associates. We have discussed investing in a cinematic project over the years. We want to finance a movie about the Nosferati. But not a horror film. One sympathetic to the Undead. As I told you, I have been favorably struck by the creativity you have shown as an auteur. I would be very happy if you would consider such a project."

I looked over at Willa. She was smiling at me.

Here I was, a kind of down-and-out writer, producer and director. I hadn't been able to drum up a dime from my former backers. And here was someone I had barely met proposing an investment in my talent. There was only one place to start. The deal.

"How much money do you and your associates have to invest in a movie project?" I asked.

"How much would be required?" he responded.

I knew what would be needed at a minimum. Maximums are hard to know until well into a production.

I told him the minimum, and told him there was always the possibility of major over-runs.

He didn't bat an eye.

"Do you have an idea of the general plot line you and your friends have in mind?" I asked.

"Yes, I do," he answered. "And it is novel enough to be quite a writing challenge. The picture I and my associates want made is about a Nosferata. A lady who has chosen our lifestyle. We want her to be sympathetically portrayed. A woman with real compassion towards others, mortals and Nosferati alike."

I caught a snippet from what he had said. "A lady who has chosen *our* lifestyle." Whose lifestyle? Was this joker who was offering to sink millions of dollars in a vampire movie trying to tell me *he* was a vampire…a Nosferatu? Come on. Give me a break.

"I've got to ask you a question, Radu," I ventured. "Give it to me straight. Are you trying to tell me *you* are a vam…a Nosferatu?"

"I know it is difficult for a mortal to understand, Mister Roberts. But I assure you, such is the case."

I cannot describe the astonishment I felt at his statement. I was glad I hadn't sampled his brandy. I needed to be stone cold sober to process his statement.

I looked over at Willa. She nodded "yes."

Yes what? Yes this guy with the diamond stickpin was a spook of some kind? Or a nut? or what?

She clarified the nod.

"Rob. I know this is going to be a shock. And I would understand if you went storming out of here feeling you were the butt of some ghastly practical joke. But all of us here this evening, except you, have joined the ranks of the Undead."

I couldn't deal sensibly with that. I had to get out of there. I had to get down off the hill to where reality as I knew it was still located.

I stood.

"Radu," I said. "My mind isn't able to deal with what you have just told me. And Willa. Your statement bowls me over even more. I guess I don't even know what a Nosferatu actually is. But I can't discuss making a film about you people, whatever you are. Not yet. Not until my brain can deal with it."

"I understand," Radu said. "This is a reality you didn't realize even existed. Are you all right to drive home?"

I assured him I was.

Willa arose and put a hand on my shoulder.

"Rob," she said. "I can see you're distressed. I probably should have prepared you somewhat for this. Go home. Think over what you've seen and heard. If you'd like to get clarification about our kind, I have a cellphone. Call me and I'll come to your place and tell you what we Nosferati are. We are not what you probably imagine."

My ex-wife, a woman I still loved, was a vampire with a cellphone? Had the world gone mad?

She wrote her phone number on a card and slipped it in my pocket.

I took my leave of Radu. Willa walked me to the door. Clement let me out.

Somehow I got back to my digs without an accident. I decided on a good stiff drink, got into bed, and managed to get to sleep.

The next day I stewed constantly about my experiences at the castle. First and foremost were thoughts about Willa. She had said she was a vampire, or, to use the word those folks up on the hill seemed to prefer, a Nosferata. Yep, I figured it out all by myself. Male Vampire = Nosferatu. Female Vampire = Nosferata. Plural Vampires = Nosferati. So much for the language lesson.

It was possible that she'd gone crazy and just hallucinated that she was a spook. If so, Radu, and probably the whole castleful, were nutty as well. Or perhaps they were all sane and I had gone bonkers.

Another possibility was that Nosferati were real, were dwelling in a castle up above Mulholland Drive, and were all really nice people.

Sure, they might sleep all day in coffins, grow fangs, and go around sucking blood out of people's necks. But, all in all, just good folks.

The whole thing really had me going cuckoo. I had to get a grip on it. What to do?

There was only one solution. Willa said she'd explain it all to me if I asked her to. I had to get a better idea from her about what she had said she had become. And about what Radu, Maurice, Marlene, Tex, Rock, and the others had become.

About noon I gave her a ring. No answer. Why didn't she answer? Why wasn't her cellphone on?

Then it struck me. If my ex-wife was really a vampire, or even if she just thought she was, she wouldn't be answering her cellphone at noon. She'd be lying dead in her coffin. Jesus Christ! What a revolting development *that* was. It made me even more concerned and dismayed.

For the rest of the day, I was really in a state. I could hardly wait for sundown.

When the sun set, I waited a while. How long does it take a vampire, or someone who thinks she's a vampire, to raise the coffin lid, stretch a bit, hop out of the box, and go brush her fangs? Does such a being descend down into the Village to breakfast on the blood of some unsuspecting tourist?

When I called this time, Willa answered.

"Rob," she said. "I'm so glad you called. I was really worried about you. It was thoughtless of me not to anticipate how shocked you would be with the realization there is a world up here on the hill that you hadn't even imagined."

I told her it had taken me by surprise all right. And that I was still confused. I reminded her she had said she would come to my place again, this time to fill me in on what was really going on.

"Would seven o'clock this evening be convenient?" she asked.

Seven wasn't very far away. I told her it would suit me just fine.

At seven she was at my door. This time she was less formal than before. I got a good hug and a kiss on the cheek.

Lord! Was I ever glad to see her. And to feel her presence in the hug and the kiss.

We sat down.

"I'd offer you something to drink," I started out. "But I gather you folks don't drink like…normal folks."

She laughed good-naturedly.

"Would it make you uncomfortable if I told you what we *do* drink?" she asked.

"Let me guess," I said. "I think I'd rather guess than hear you say it."

She crossed her legs, sat back relaxed, and said, "Go ahead, Rob. That suits your style exactly."

"Blood," I said.

She nodded.

"Human blood," I embellished, to make sure of what we were talking about.

"Good for you, Rob," she said. "There's nothing like clearing up the dicey points first."

"And, to get your drink, may I ask? Do you happen to have grown fangs?"

"Would you like to see?" she asked.

I really didn't want to see, just in case it was true. And yet, I *had* to see in order to deal with it. If it was true.

"The fangs are retractable," she said. "And they emerge when I get excited. If you'll let me get close to you where I can catch the scent of your blood and your hormones, it will happen."

I know my face showed something between fascination and horror.

"Blood and sex scents turn you on? Fangwise?" I kind of blurted.

"Yes, that's how it happens," she said. "So if you really want to see how it works, I need to get close to you. But don't worry, Rob. I won't bite. I promise."

A promise from my ex-wife the vampire woman. Vampiress? Whatever. I trusted her. And I wanted to have her next to me.

"Come on, Baby," I said cavalierly. "Show me what ya' got."

"Stay seated," she advised.

She got up and nuzzled me cheek to cheek. She rubbed lips around my neck. And I'll be damned if I didn't sprout an erection.

She stepped away from me and said, "See? Convinced?"

Damned if she didn't have sharp fangs where her eyeteeth should have been. And I'll tell you God's truth. They were sexy, gorgeous, and turned me on.

She went back to her chair and sat down.

She flashed me a big smile and said, "When that bulge in your pants goes down and you stop filling the air with your musky testosterone scent, the fangs will retract."

We sat quietly for a while as I gradually became less aroused. And when that happened, the fangs slithered back up into her mouth.

"Well I'll be a monkey's uncle," I said.

For the next several hours she had a lot of explaining to do. The first hurdle had been cleared. She had made me a believer that she was, indeed, a Nosferata. I was dazed. And if I wasn't so crazy about her, I would have been aghast.

But I realized I still loved the woman, fanged or unfanged. And, she certainly did look cute and sexy with those two gleaming little tusks.

She told me Rock Stone had learned about the Nosferati from one of the many friends he had made during his party-giving days. He had become Undead to keep his good looks and for the sex. It seems Maurice and Rock were lovers. Maurice became transfigured by Rock quite willingly.

Willa and Maurice had divorced because Maurice was much more interested in chasing boys than in staying her husband. But, before they separated, she had decided to join the lifestyle (Undeathstyle?)

She explained about the difference between mortals, Voevods, and Nosferati. She explained that Nosferati never sought blood from mortals unless the mortal requested it. Although this fact was counterintuitive to me I accepted it. She even told me about the bloodbank at the Transibar, but at the time didn't tell me the bloodbank's source.

She told me about purakh and how one can only become Undead by the infusion of the substance through the fangs of a Nosferatu.

She related the feelings of sexual ecstasy that are felt by Nosferatu and Voevod alike while having fanged sex. I thought of her fangs and knew that was something I would love.

I began by propositioning my own ex-wife.

"Suppose I told you, Darling, that I would be delighted if you were to treat me to the experience you just described?"

"I would have to say, 'Tell me. Don't ask'."

"All right," I countered. "Willa, you lovely fanged temptress. You Vamp. I want you to sink your fangs into my neck and suck, suck,

suck."

"Oh, you old Romeo," she laughed. "You *do* have a way with words. Let's go into your boudoir, disrobe, and I'll do you a suck you won't forget."

I could hardly walk upright into my bedroom. I had a very insistent erection.

Back when I was married to Willa, I had been absolutely faithful to her. Oh, I flirted a bit. And copped a feel whenever I thought I could get away with it. With my power to cast female parts in my productions, even bit parts, I never resorted to the casting couch. I was happy in my marriage and was in love with my wife.

After our divorce, I hardly led a celibate life. I was available and women were available. There is very little prudery in our town.

I was fond of all the women I slept with. I really like women. But when it comes to love, I found that I was a one-woman man. And in my pettiness, I had driven that woman away.

Here my woman had returned to me. She had divorced the "great French lover." She was free. I was free. What we were about to engage in would be a new tie, a blood wedding. I believed it would prove to be truly holy and binding.

As we undressed, I could not take my eyes off that form I knew so well and idolized completely. Her preternatural pallor became her. She was like a lovely Greek statue come to life. That radiant face with its classic cheekbones. Those breasts that spelled perfect womanhood. A midriff made for nuzzling. Her mons veneris with its russet triangle. Legs, feet, yes, even toes — perfection.

She turned away for a moment and I drank in that delightful derrière I was wild to clasp into my aching palms.

"God, Willa," I said. "I love you so much. You'll never know how much I missed you."

She came up to me, took my face in her hands, and whispered, "I know, Love. Me too. But let's not talk. Let's not relive the past. Let us live only these moments, right now."

I lifted her off her feet, carried her to the bed, and laid her atop the covers.

I lay down next to her and just feasted my eyes on her loveliness.

My right hand found purchase on her midriff. My lips followed my hand and I found myself tracing circles around her navel with my tongue.

I had to look up to see her reaction. Those two precious denticles gave testimony to her arousal.

I nuzzled my way from her midriff to her alabaster orbs. Each rosy nipple had arisen to receive my flicking tongue and playful nibbles.

She took my face in her hands as she had before and raised me up to where we were face-to-face. She played soft sweet touches about my lips.

I kissed her on the mouth, getting the feel for those fangs that would enter me as I entered her. Not yet. Not yet.

My hand descended to her crotch, and her hand took gentle hold on my phallus. As she gently manipulated me, my fingers sought the glory of her clitoris.

"Now is the moment, My Dear," she told me.

She caused me to lie flat on my back on the bed. Her mouth hovered over my neck. She raised her hips, straddled me, and as she descended, enveloping my penis with her fragrant vagina, her teeth penetrated the skin of my neck and pierced into the artery there.

I cannot describe the sensation. Pain? Yes, undoubtedly. Not worldly pain, but exquisite, blessed pangs. The burning transformed into ardor and a feeling of elation coursed through my bloodstream from the crown of my head to the tips of my toes. And the verve concentrated on the spot where we were joined together genitally. Fangs to neck, penis to vagina, belly to belly, we were engaged in our blood wedding.

I had had sexual experiences from my first flush of puberty. In school I always had compliant girlfriends. I thought I had found the epitome of sexual satisfaction in bed with the woman I loved and married. But this ceremony of the blood wedding went so far beyond my previous experiences that words fail me in attempting to describe it. And it continued on, and on, and on. A continuous Nirvana.

Willa drew my blood very slowly. It took hours before she had to cease in order not to debilitate me from blood loss.

When her fangs retracted, and my manhood became flaccid again, we lay next to each other, hand-in-hand, smiling idiotically at the ceiling.

Willa and Rob were truly reunited.

Time came to get out of bed and get dressed. Willa was satiated. I was thirsty as Hell.

We went into the kitchen. I brewed myself a cup of coffee. She silently watched me drink it.

"If we're going to do much of this from now on, I've got to keep oysters here in my fridge," I joked.

"You'd better corner the market, Chum," she answered. "We've only just begun."

I was now a Voevod with a common-law vampire wife. We went up to the castle to talk to Radu about the movie he wanted to make. I could not have been more enthusiastic about the project.

It was understood that I would remain a Voevod at least until the project was completed and the picture released. I would not be able to produce and direct a motion picture if I had to lie in a casket all day long. Even if we would be doing all the shooting at night. Which I proposed we do. When the project was out and distributed, perhaps I would accept the immortality of the purakh. But for the time being, Willa and I lived in the moment, not in the future.

I worked by day. We partied by night. Willa and I *did* Hollywood as we had never done it before. I did all the drinking. She found the champagne as she savored my blood. We were probably the happiest couple in Hollywood.

I had no problem striking a deal with Olympic Studios. When I demonstrated that I had financial backers with deep pockets, the welcome mat appeared back at the studio door, even when I told them the shooting would all be done at night. After all, I wanted to use some of the talent from up in the castle as cast members.

Rock Stone would be the male lead. But we had to discard that old male starlet name. The name on his birth certificate was Albert Masters. We decided to do the unusual by Hollywood standards and use his real name in the credits.

Karl Tepes was allowed the part of the heroine's sister Camilla. Since he would be playing in drag, he couldn't use his screen name. He retained his birth name, Carol, and tweaked his family name, Giurescu, into Juress. Marlene got a part and... Oh, what the Hell. Go see the movie and find out for yourself.

What we did not have was anyone suitable for the role of the Vamp, Veronica. She had to be young, pale, blonde, and beautiful. She had to look innocent up on the screen even when she was wearing fangs and sucking blood from her lover.

I spent hours with agents looking for the right young lady to play Veronica. We were up to the moment when we were ready to begin our first nighttime shoot.

And we still lacked a leading lady.

THE VOICE OF LIBBE BONTE

Mama said we would have to go to Hollywood for me to get "discovered." Monon, Indiana was home, but no one was discovering me there.

We never had lots of money back in Monon. Mama was a waitress at Spanky's Café and she got good tips because she's real friendly and the truckers who stop there for breakfast could joke with her and she joked back.

But even with a steady job working in the morning shift and getting those tips, we were, well, kind of poor.

But Mama had a dream. Her dream was for me to be discovered when I got to be eighteen. She put money into a special account at The Peoples Bank downtown every week.

"When the time comes, and you're eighteen, we'll have enough money in that account to go West, where you can get discovered."

I'd heard her say that for as long as I could remember. And "West" meant only one thing. Hollywood.

I was happy in Monon. I liked school a lot. I was good in all my subjects, especially English and History. As far as I was concerned, I would have been happy to go on to Valparaiso College after high school and learn to be a teacher. I didn't dare tell Mama, though. She was determined for me to get discovered. And that was that.

I graduated from Monon High with real good grades. The counselor there urged me to go on to college. She said I had the makings of being a scholar. She even tried to get me to apply for a scholarship at Valparaiso.

But I never said anything to Mama about all that. Her mind was determined what she wanted my destiny to be. And that, as I've told you, was to get me discovered.

That bank account she had kept growing and growing. And, just as she'd planned, by the time I was a senior at high school, there was enough money in the account for us to pull up stakes and head West in the Ford.

Mama's boss, Steve, from the café, threw us a real nice going-away party. The regular customers and lots of the truckers came. Everyone was real nice and encouraging. They wished us well and said I was sure to get discovered. Everyone knew Mama's dream and seemed to think it was realizable.

I didn't really doubt it. I could look in the mirror. And I could see that I was pretty. I liked being pretty. But I got tired of people always harping on how attractive I was. They didn't have to tell me. I knew. And I knew that it was the way I looked rather than my brains that would get me discovered.

Our trip out to California was pretty uneventful. There wasn't much on the way that impressed me enough to make me want to go back and see it again. And Mama didn't want to stop much. Her goal was Hollywood, and she pressed the pedal to the metal pretty much to get us there as soon as she could.

When we got to Hollywood, first off, Mama found us a neat place to stay. The Castello Hotel is located on Franklin near Highland, close to all the sights she longed to see. The price was right. We had plenty of room and an adequate kitchen. The kitchen was important to keep our costs down. And the place even had a swimming pool that I loved.

We walked a *lot*. We had to stand at the corner of Hollywood and Vine. Why? There's nothing much to see there. But Mama had always heard that Hollywood and Vine was "where it's at." So we had to be there.

Grauman's Chinese Theater was more interesting. We hung around its entry court for hours studying all the stars' hand and foot prints and signatures in the cement. We'd check our own hands and feet against theirs. There must be over a hundred and fifty different stars' prints there. That kept us pretty busy.

Then we spent hours and hours along that Hollywood Walk of Fame. Bronze medallions in the sidewalk with the names of so-called stars. Most of them were people I'd never heard of. But Mama went nuts over them.

We had to take the tour of the movie stars' homes, and all that.

We were seeing a lot of Hollywood, but I wasn't getting discovered.

Schwab's drugstore where some star a long time ago got discovered wasn't there any more. Mama had bought me a sweater just to wear in there.

I thought it was all a lot less interesting and exciting than Mama did. But as much as she liked it, nothing was happening to get me discovered. And Mama began to get a little discouraged.

We had left Monon in June. All summer long we kept trying to find an agent. No agency even returned Mama's calls. September rolled around. Schools started. Still nothing. It wasn't until November that my chance came. And it came right out of the blue. Or, I should say, right out of the dark.

One of the places Mama took me to get me discovered was the Cinespace at Hollywood Boulevard and Ivar.

She heard that the real movie addicts swarm there. And that turned out to be right. It's a restaurant, and the food is good. But the big draw is that they show films there Wednesdays through Saturdays. So you eat in the dark while watching older movies. Later, after the show, there's a D.J. and dancing. But Mama and I never stayed for that. I thought that the dance floor might be a good place for me to get discovered. But Mama didn't like us being at a dance without gentlemen escorts.

This one night, it was the Thursday a week before Thanksgiving, we went to the Cinespace a little early so we could order and get our first course served before they turned out the lights.

There was a double feature that evening. The program on our table gave us some background about the movies. Both were directed by Tod Browning. One was silent, called *London After Midnight* and the other was a talkie called *The Mark of the Vampire.* Exactly the same story, but with different actors, naturally. And in the first one the only sound was the music.

Across the room there was a couple that I noticed. The reason I noticed was that they were staring at me. I'd catch them at it and they would look away. I'd glance over and catch them at it again. I was used to guys staring at me. I can toss that off easily. But a couple?

Mama and I were still eating our salads when the lights went out and the first film started. I got wrapped up in the vampire stuff and forgot all about the rude couple.

We finished our salads in the dark and got served our next course by waiters who must be able to see in the dark. I don't know how they do it.

When the lights came on after the first picture so they could change the reels, I could feel that same couple looking at me. This time it kind of gave me the chills. The vampire movie had been spooky enough without having a couple of weirdos checking you out. Jeesh!

I liked the next movie better. I mean, it was the same plot but I recognized the actors and they were talking. Bela Lugosi was in it and I'd seen him in *Dracula* on late night movies on TV. And Lionel Barrymore was in it. And he's in enough of the re-runs they do on television that I knew him, too.

When the lights came on after the show, that couple I talked about headed for our able. I have to admit, I got kind of scared.

The man handed Mama his business card.

"Excuse me for interrupting," he said. "I'm Rob Roberts, a film producer here in town."

Mama nearly jumped up and shook the guy's hand.

He told us he was casting for a vampire movie he was producing and that he thought I might be just right for an important part. He asked if I could come over to Olympic Studios the next morning at ten o'clock for a screen test.

Mama answered "yes" for me.

This Mister Roberts wrote down our names and telephone number on a notepad he had in his pocket.

And guess what? I'd been discovered.

The screen test turned out fine. Mister Roberts signed me to a contract. I would be playing the lead, Veronica, in a movie called *Vamp.*

I was happy that I had really landed a job in the movies. A leading role. Mama was even happier. This had always been her dream, not mine. So, above all, I was happy that I had made her happy.

There was one funny thing about the way the picture was shot. It was only done after dark. Mister Roberts said that was because it was a vampire movie and all the action would seem more authentic if it was shot at night.

That seemed kind of screwy to me because it was all shot indoors anyway. They could make it as dark or as bright as they wanted.

But who was I to complain? Mister Roberts wrote the script, he produce the movie, and he directed it. So what he said went. I was getting a nice salary and I was making Mama happy. So why make a thing of whether I was working daytime or nighttime?

The cast members, cameramen, costume people – all the kinds of people you meet on the set – were friendly folks who were nice to me.

I gradually got the feeling that some of the actors I was working with were different. I don't just mean different from the folks back in Monon. Of course they were different from them. They were famous Hollywood actors. But they were different from everyone. It's hard to explain.

I had to sleep in the daytime and work at night. I fell into that pattern pretty easily. But Mama just couldn't manage to sleep during the day. She had to be out and busy. So, although she came to the studio with me in the evenings, she was back at our place on Franklin and was in bed long before we finished shooting in the early hours of the morning.

Mister Roberts' wife kind of took over as a mother figure when Mama wasn't around. I say his "wife," but she was really his ex-wife. But they'd gotten together again somehow. It's one of those Hollywood arrangements you'd hardly ever see back in Monon.

She wanted me to call her Willa, which suited me fine. She talked to me a lot at first about the premise of the picture. How it depicted vampires, and most of the time they're referred to as "Nosferati," as basically good people with a lifestyle that is just different from mortals. And the part I was playing, Veronica, was a Nosferata who was kind, compassionate and loving. But who was misunderstood and discriminated against by mortals.

Gradually Willa hinted that there really were Nosferati in the world. And that they were good, decent people. I began to think that in Hollywood there were clearly all types. So why not Nosferati? I tried to explain that to Mama, who had a real hard time even listening to such an idea.

Finally, along about March, when the filming was really going good and I knew everyone on the set pretty well, Willa told me she herself was a Nosferata. Now that one really shocked me. When I told Mama, she just about wigged out.

Naturally Mama asked Willa about it. And bit by bit accepted that it *was* true. And since she liked Willa a lot, like I did, that made Nosferati nearly all right in her book. But she was still pretty leery.

The next shocker was when Willa told me my leading man, Albert Masters, was one. Albert? I was about to say something stupid like "but he's too handsome to be a vampire." But, of course, Willa is a beautiful woman. And she's a…Vamp. And that really famous actress we have in the picture as my aunt, Marlene Grabo? Guess what? She's one too. And quite a few more of the actors were Nosferati.

I got used to the idea. And eventually Mama did too. But not as much as me. She wasn't with them as much as I was and didn't really get to know any of them very personally, except maybe Willa.

In late April, Willa told me the Nosferati were going to throw a party up at a castle on the hill where they all live. Would I like to go?

It was going to be on May fourth, a kind of big party day for them. I talked it over with Mama. The party was scheduled to last all night. But those of us who were just regular people would be expected to leave before midnight. I understood that. The later hours would be for a more intimate party with their own kind.

Mama had grown accustomed to the fact that she now knew some genuine, bona fide vampires. And she was comfortable with me going to the party if Willa and Mister Roberts were going to be there to chaperone me.

But she was uncomfortable about going to a castle full of vampires herself. Even with Willa and Mister Roberts there.

So, she let me go alone.

And it proved to be just *wonderful*.

CHAPTER FIVE

ENTER FREELY AND OF YOUR OWN WILL

THE VOICE OF TIM AXELROD

When Carol had written asking me to try to get home to Hollywood for at least a three day stay on May second, third, and fourth, it was that last day that piqued my interest the most.

It was May fourth, the feast day of Saint Judas Cyrianus. Carol was about as irreligious a person as I knew. She promised a grand party to honor that saint I'd never even heard of. Yet, to tell the truth, I don't know about many saints anyway.

The day had arrived. I had met the host of the party, Prince Radu Frumos Dracula, at the Transibar the day before. And I was convinced he was a very real manifestation of the preternatural creatures I was writing about in my master's thesis. And he turned me on mightily.

I had learned that this saint that Carol had written about was a goddam vampire, too. And the patron saint of the whole fucking bunch.

I doubted that any of this would be allowable in my thesis. But what the Hell? I was going to go to a vampire party and maybe get sucked by my favorite vampire.

I knew the drill about getting myself up to Summit Drive. I knew what kind of dragon figure to look for on a brass plate. I'd seen one already down in West Hollywood. Seen one, you've seen 'em all.

I got myself up the hill in the old Honda Civic. Sure enough, the brass plate with the scary dragon was attached to a gate. I used the callbox and got through the gate. I drove up the one-lane road to the castle.

Yep, it sure looked like a set from a 1930s movie.

I found the bell and rang.

Who should greet me but a character out of one of Tod Browning's old flicks. It was a joker with a broken neck who looked like he belonged in an Addams Family sitcom or in an Abbot and Costello Meet the Vampire type movie.

What does the guy greet me with? That old chestnut, "Enter freely and of your own will."

"Boy," I thought. "This party's gonna really be a pisser."

I got inside this giant room and Radu spied me immediately. He was with a very thin, exquisitely beautiful broad. I'd come up here with the hots for the guy's body. And, all signs were that he was straight and already had his squeeze for the night.

Jesus! Was *that* ever a downer.

He and the babe came over to greet me. She was Countess Somethingorother. What she really was, was the signpost to me: "You ain't fucking *this* prince tonight, Sonny. He's mine." I got pretty good at reading those kind of signs up at Stanford.

While the prince and the goddam countess were welcoming me, I spotted Karl. He was there as Carol, in a black evening gown with a slit up the side to show off her fabulous left leg. She was with a big blond hunk of a guy.

Carol and the Hunk came over to greet me. The Hunk was introduced as Albert Whatsisface or something. I could tell that Carol was taken for the night, too. Prince with Countess plus Carol with Whatshisface seemed to equal no sex tonight for the dude from Palo Alto. Hell! After all, Carol had invited me to this shindig in the first place. No way to treat a pal. And I was even going to let the prince sink his pearlies into my jugular for some of that old vampire action. Shit!

Carol told the Prince she and Hunk would introduce me around. I could tell Carol and Hunkface would be inseparable. Like they were joined at the hip. Or someplace else.

There were some people there I actually knew. I knew Willa and Rob Roberts from the studio. I had seen Marlene Grabo and Maurice Delatour in the movies. There were others I either knew or had seen on the silver screen too.

Then Carol steered me up to a gal who absolutely took my breath away. Do you believe in love at first sight? I didn't up until then, myself. This babe was gorgeous. She had a beautiful face and body. But shining through her there beamed a real intelligence.

"Tim, I'd like you to meet Libbe Bonte," Carol said. "She's playing the lead in Rob's latest flick down at Olympic. Libbe, this is an old friend of mine, Tim Axelrod. You know his Uncle Mike Axelrod who's the set designer for the show we're filming. And he's also a good friend of your friend Tilly Blaine, who does all your costumes."

I stumbled through some sort of stupid greeting. What I wanted was for Carol and her hunk to go get lost. Carol seemed to have the same idea, because she said, "You two have something in common here tonight. Everyone else is either a Nosferatu or a Voevod. You two are the only mortals around the place. You should have a lot to talk about."

With that Carol skipped off with her boyfriend.

As it turned out, Libbe and I *did* have a lot in common. She was well-read and bright. When I told her I had come down from Stanford for the party, she asked what I was studying there. Before long we were on to contemporary vampire novels like Anne Rice's and Elizabeth Kostova's. We shared our surprise at recently learning that the Undead really did exist, and that we were in a castle surrounded by them.

In the first half-hour I became a changed man. More transformed than any of the other people partying in the castle. I knew that I had just passed out of my bisexual phase. I wouldn't have thought that possible. But it was true.

I was in LOVE. In love with the woman I would give everything to be with for the rest of my lie.

And I could feel that she responded to me. Maybe not as wildly as I did to her. But there was hope.

Her movie would be released in few months. And she would immediately become a famous movie star.

I would have to complete a few more years at Stanford to get my doctorate. Then I would become a professor. I knew I had the stuff to make it in academia.

I asked her if she thought she would ever agree to become a Voevod or a Nosferata.

"Never, Tim," she said with conviction. "I don't want to remain an actress all my life. I don't have to keep looking like I'm eighteen forever. After a couple more movies, I will have satisfied my mother's need to have a daughter who's made it in the movies. I will want to settle down then and have a normal life. The idea of getting bitten in the neck and having otherworldly sex is, frankly, a turn-off to me.

That was the woman I loved.

We sought out Carol and then Radu to thank them and to take our leave. We were out of the castle by ten-thirty.

We had to drive our separate cars down the hill.

I told her I'd call her the next day and hoped we could get together.

She said she hoped so, too.

When I got back to Stanford, I wrote my thesis, leaving out everything I'd learned in my three day trip home. I'm working on my doctoral dissertation now on…what else? Myth and folklore.

Libbe's made three movies since we met. She's the toast of Hollywood.

But when I come home for the holidays and school breaks, she always manages to drop everything to be with me.

Can a famous movie actress find love and happiness as the wife of a college professor?

I certainly hope so.

APPENDICES TO
DRACULA SUCKS HOLLYWOOD DUDES

APPENDIX I

RADU AND VLAD

Vlad Tepes Dracula was born in 1431 in Sighisoara, Romania, which is in the Transylvania Province of that country. Vlad is a name common to many members of his family.

Tepes means "Impaler." The name was given as an epithet due to his fame for impaling vampires who were enemies of his province or of his rule.

He had learned in Turkey how to destroy vampires who were a threat to the state. The method involves driving an aspen or ashtree stake through the vampire's rectum, on up through the heart, and out the mouth. It must not be driven directly through the chest and into the heart as some folktales suggest.

The vampire's legs are tied to horses that pull the thighs apart so the stake can be carefully inserted. The practice is painless since it is performed in broad daylight when the Undead are not conscious. The term Tepes was bestowed as an honorific by his people, since Vlad was and remains a Romanian military hero. Dispensing of Undead adversaries was seen as a benefit to the state.

Vlad was both a general and a prince of Wallachia-Transylvania. He fought off incursions of the Turks and the Hungarians. He suppressed insurgencies of the Saxons residing in his domain. He was honored in life and in death as the Christian savior of his people.

Vlad avenged the death of his father and older brother by arranging for the death of the Hungarian boyar, John Hunyadi. He was later captured by Hungarian forces and imprisoned in the city of Buda on the Danube from 1448 to 1456. His brothers Radu and Mircea ruled his province in his absence, under the protection of the Ottoman sultan. Vlad was freed from captivity in 1475 and returned to Wallachia-Transylvania as prince. His brothers happily relinquished rule to him.

In 1476, Vlad became disenchanted with the Christian cause for which he had fought all his life. He came to the decision that Islam was the one true religion. Just as he had been a Christian extremist all his life to that time, he now became a Moslem extremist. He faked his own death by having a fallen Wallachian army officer buried under his name at the monastery on Snagov Island, which is in one of the lakes near Bucharest. His so-called tomb is much visited by tourists to this day.

Vlad made his way to Istanbul in 1476 and offered his services to Sultan Mohammed II. He submitted to becoming a vampire that year and served the Ottoman Empire as well as the other Islamic nations from that time on as advisor to the many jihads or holy wars that have erupted throughout that region since the time of the Christian Crusades.

He has recently assumed the name Osama bin Laden and carries out his extremist views on an international scale.

Vlad Tepes Dracula was the model for Bram Stoker's Victorian novel *Dracula*. He has been depicted since in novels and cinema as a monster. He remains a hero to Romanians and to those Turks who know of his assistance to Islam following his feigned death.

One of Vlad's younger brothers was Radu Frumos Dracula, who was born in 1438. Radu was, and is, a common Romanian given name. Frumos, meaning "The Handsome," was applied as an epithet from a very early age since he was (and is) uncommonly good looking. He became a vampire in 1455 while a hostage in Turkey. He remained in Turkey until 1448 when he returned to his homeland to serve as prince along with his younger brother Mircea.

Mircea, who had become a monk, left his order to serve with Radu as ruler, since Radu was unavailable for any functions from sunrise to sunset. The two brothers looked similar enough that the deception was never noticed by their people.

In 1474, with his brother back on the Wallachian throne, Radu returned to the Ottoman Empire and to the Island of Samos where he had previously ruled. In 1480, he left Samos and spent his time traveling and learning. His brother Mircea returned to the cloistered life of a monk upon Vlad's return to power.

Radu was never extreme in religion like his older brother. Never really either a practicing Christian or Moslem, he was, and is, a secular humanist.

In the eighteenth century, he participated in the French Revolution.

In the early twentieth century, he became a Communist.

When he became disenchanted with that cause, after seeing the effect of Communist rule in his native Romania, he went to Hollywood and resides there to this day.

APPENDIX II

HISTORICAL OVERVIEW OF THE SPREAD OF VAMPIRISM

There were vampires dwelling in the Indus Valley of the Indian subcontinent in prehistoric times. They constructed the community of Mohenjo-Daro prior to the building of the pyramids of Egypt. Their dwellings were more comfortable than any prehistoric excavations uncovered to date anywhere. They are the only known people in prehistoric times to have constructed a sanitary toilet system that flushed their waste into the sea.

How they came to have purakh (the bread of eternal life) flowing through their veins is unknown. Probably it was an evolutionary phenomenon in response to their environment over millennia.

They dwelt peacefully, satisfying their need for human blood as sustenance by agreements with mortals living in their proximity. There is no reason to believe they ever ingested the blood of mortals uninvited.

The Vanijah, for that is the name they were given when the Caucasian invaders of India introduced the alphabet, survived two conquests of the subcontinent. They were never relegated to the untouchable caste by the conquerors.

However, when India was conquered by the Islamic Moguls, travel through Islam was accessible to all. Roads led from Mohenjo-Daro to Madras, and Madras to Delhi. From Delhi to Baghdad. From Baghdad to Turkistan. Thus the Vanijah gradually forsook their homeland of Mohenjo-Daro and spread throughout Islam into the Turkish Ottoman Empire.

The Vanijah, who were later called Vampyr, and later still Nosferati, are found today on every occupied continent. They often find work that has to be done at night, since they become very weak when exposed to daylight.

APPENDIX III

BLOODY MATTERS

Perhaps the best recognized characteristic of vampirism is its connection with blood. In order to survive, a vampire must drink blood. In the truest tradition, the blood must be human.

Nosferati gourmets develop preferences for blood types. In each type, there are plus and minus sub-classifications, indicating the presence or absence of its Rhesus factor. The great majority of humans are Rh+.

The ten most common blood types in humans are: O, A, B, RzRz, Jk, DI, U, Vel, and Dr. Each of these, of course, is sub-classified as + or − to indicate the Rhesus factor.

Of all blood types, Nosferati most favor DI+, known by hematologists as Diego type. It comes only from Native Americans and East Asians. Latin Americans with strong Amerindian genes and Tonkinese from Southeast Asia are prime sources for the blood type in Southern California.

Prince Radu Fromos Dracula, a Hollywood-based businessman, is the prime purveyor of Diego type blood in North America. He owns two mortuaries in Southern California. One is in the Boyle Heights neighborhood of Los Angeles, home to a large Latin American population. The mortuary is known for the excellence of its cosmetology. When blood is drained from the veins of the dearly departed prior to the introduction of formaldehyde, it is separated by blood-type and transported to the cellars of the Transibar, a cocktail lounge owned by the prince.

The prince's other mortuary is located in the Los Angeles suburb of Westchester, home to the largest contingent of Tonkinese in North America. The procedures used at the Boyle Heights mortuary prevail in Westchester.

All blood types are available at the Transibar on Alta Loma Road in West Hollywood. Diego type is the most expensive. Blood is also served at all Nosferatu parties in the world. Diego type blood, however, is generally reserved for gala events.

APPENDIX IV

MAILAMUNTE CASTLE

People driving around in the Hollywood Hills will eventually find Mulholland Drive. Looking up from where Mulholland Drive, Laurel Canyon Boulevard, and Woodrow Wilson Drive converge, if you crane your neck you can catch a glimpse of Summit Drive.

At Summit Drive there is a gated road. On the gate is a dragon emblem and a callbox.

From that spot, a large private mansion in the shape of an East European castle is barely visible atop the hill. It occasions wonder by the vagabond motorist who has arrived at the location.

There is a certain amount of Hollywood history surrounding that castle.

Otto Caruthers, who produced and directed four Dracula movies at Olympic Studios, purchased the site back when his first vampire movie, *Vampires at the O.K. Corral*, was being filmed. He hired Hans Panoldi, the famous Northern California architect to draw up plans for a castle that would look like the castle in Tod Browning's 1931 production, *Dracula*.

Caruthers lost interest in the project and sold both the lot and the plans to Clement Robles, who was a major investor in many of his films, including the monster flicks.

Robles was not only a Hollywood investor but also a very successful drug dealer who catered to Hollywood's inexhaustible craving for cocaine. Robles actually had the castle built. He was later convicted of kidnapping and was hanged in San Quentin prison.

However, before his conviction, he sold the property to a Romanian prince. It is said that Robles, a gentleman of Latin extraction, had a rare blood type known as Diego.

Superstitious gossip in Hollywood claims that the so-called prince was a vampire who transformed Robles into an Undead, so the apparent execution at San Quentin did not actually kill the man. It is further alleged that Clement Robles is currently the majordomo at the castle.

A further twist on the story: Grave robbers are said to have stolen Robles body from its grave. The body has never been found. Speculation has it that the body was sold to Stanford Medical School for spare parts.

APPENDIX V

VAMPYR

In 1931, Tod Browning produced the talking picture *Dracula* at Universal Studios in Hollywood. It was based on a play which in turn was based on Bram Stoker's novel, *Dracula*. It was the first of the scores of talking pictures about vampires.

Bela Lugosi, a Hungarian actor, had played the part of the count on Broadway to critical acclaim. He was chosen for the title role in the film and remains the image of Dracula in the minds of movie goers everywhere.

The following year, 1932, Carl Dreyer, a French producer, released his movie *Vampyr*. A year after its French release it appeared in America as *The Vampire* and two years later as *Castle of Doom.*

In England it was released under the title *The Strange Adventures of David Gray*. It is not based on Bram Stoker's novel but rather on the story *Carmilla* by Sheridan Le Fanu.

Among film critics of the genre it is considered the classic cinematic vampire portrayal.

APPENDIX VI

SONG OF THE MAIDEN'S BLOOD

The blood that flows through human veins
As rivers through the meads
Was jealous of the birds' sweet songs,
And said, "I too shall sing!"
The blood did covet wild wind's songs,
And said, "I too shall sing."

An evening in the month of May
At sunset's magic hour
A maiden wandering in the fields
Heard blood cry out to her.
The blood burned in her, thus it spoke
"What are you making of your youth,
"What will you make of me?
"I long to sing, I long to dance

"I would you'd think of me."

Beyond her view a stranger stood
The one who watches all.

The blood that flows through human veins
As rivers through the meads
Was jealous of the birds' sweet songs,
And said, "I too shall sing!"

ABOUT THE AUTHOR

TIM DESMONDES

Tim Desmondes was born and raised in Los Angeles. He has lived his entire life in California and has resided in many communities in that state.

Tim currently lives with his wife in a beach town in Southern California.

Tim is also the author of:

Sex and Loathing in Hollywood

Sexual Diversity and Perversity

Dracula Sucks Hollywood Dudes

Venus Does Adonis while Apollo Shags a Tree

Available at Amazon.com, TheNazcaPlainsCorp.com and your Local Bookstore